Newlywed Assassin

Royal House Series: Book 1

AE Moran

The Invisible Publishing Company

Contents

Chapter 1: Geneviève

I have to stop myself from taking a step closer to my brother Remi when we walk into the grand dining room of the Royal Palace of Monaco. The whole Royal Family is here, including Crown Prince Gustav, Princess Jasmine, and all their grown children—or almost all of them.

I've never met any of them before and I definitely have never set foot in the palace before.

"Remember what I told you," Remi growls in my ear. "Stay close to me and don't ever let yourself be alone with any of them. They're snakes—every last one of them."

I nod. My family has been going over this every ten minutes every day for weeks. I can't count the number of times someone has warned me about how rotten the Royal Family is.

My father, three brothers, and my two cousins stand on this side of the room. I'm the only female member of the Lefebvre family present.

Plenty of women stand on the Royal Family's side. Besides Princess Jasmine, her sister Marguerite and Jasmine's two daughters, Simone and Emeline, stand over there with Crown Prince Gustav and his sons, Christophe, Pascal, Renáld, and Marguerite's son and daughter, Dorian and Johanne.

The Crown Prince's nephews, Casim and Salvatore, also stand over there with their sister Daphne. The three of them came to live at the palace after their father's death ten years ago.

The Crown Prince treats the three of them as his own and they are considered as much his children as his own sons and daughters.

Of course I only know all of that from the press releases—and from my family briefing me on who I would meet at this official dinner. I've never met any of these people before, much less stood in the same room with them.

No one moves a muscle for at least a minute when my family steps into the dining room. A matching wave of tension goes through the Royal Family on their side.

I can see their reactions written all over their faces. The Crown Prince, his sons, nephews, and even his daughters and nieces narrow their eyes at my family. There's no love lost between their side and ours.

My father breaks the tension by stepping forward to greet the Crown Prince. My father stops in front of the Crown Prince and they clasp each other's hands. They don't kiss each other on the cheek nor do they hug. That would be asking too much.

"You are most welcome, my old friend," the Crown Prince begins. "Thank you for coming to meet with us. Please—introduce us to your lovely family and let's sit down like real people."

My father pretends to laugh. I could cut the tension with a knife.

They separate their hands instantly and the Crown Prince waves to his wife and oldest children. "This is my wife, the Princess Jasmine." He waves toward my father. "This is Silvain Lefebvre."

My father bows to Princess Jasmine, kisses her hand, and murmurs, "It's an honor, Your Highness."

The Crown Prince goes through the whole group and introduces Christophe as his heir. No one mentions why the Crown Prince's second oldest son is his heir.

The Crown Prince's oldest son isn't here. He's the only member of the Royal Family not present.

The Crown Prince's children and nephews greet my father just as stiffly. Then it's time for my father to introduce the Royal Family to all of us.

My father leads them over to us and starts the introductions with my oldest brother Raoul. Then my father introduces Remi, then my brother Marcel, and my two cousins, Gabriel and René.

My father comes to me last of all and the whole group stops in front of me. "This is my daughter, Geneviève, as I'm sure you know."

I curtsey to the Crown Prince as politely as I can. "The honor is all mine, Your Highness," I murmur.

He clasps my hands and lifts me to my feet. "Not at all, my dear. You are most welcome. May I introduce my son, Christophe?"

My eyes shoot to Christophe, but he's already eyeing me with the same intense hostility radiating from the whole Royal Family.

He would be good-looking if he wasn't one of them. His black hair and black eyes give him an exotic, elegant appearance.

His immaculate tuxedo doesn't hurt, either. He's almost six feet tall with a strong, athletic build and sharp, alert, flashing eyes.

His gaze flickers down to my full-length gown with the low, scoop neckline. I'm wearing a full chiffon skirt with a tight, corset top and a jeweled pendent hanging not quite all the way to my cleavage.

He takes in my whole carefully constructed appearance in one glance. I can just hear my brother Remi's words ringing in my ears for the thousandth time.

"You want to look attractive but not slutty. You want to interest him without making it seem like you're throwing yourself at him—or that we're throwing you at him."

"You are throwing me at him," I pointed out. "I never asked for this, remember?"

I take in Christophe's expression in one glance. He's as displeased with this arrangement as I am. His father is probably making him go through with it to seal the peace between our families.

Neither Christophe nor I get a chance to say a word before the Crown Prince waves toward the big dining table. It's set for all of us to sit down and have dinner.

"Let's sit down," the Crown Prince suggests. "I'm sure we can discuss this in a civilized manner and come to an agreement."

Our family advances into the room and spreads around the table. My brothers and cousins get even more agitated when the palace butlers and servants try to show us to our seats.

My designated seat is in the middle of the table near Johanne, Simone, and Emeline. Remi flares up immediately. "They're trying to separate you from us." He gets in the butler's face. "Put her down here with us. No, she's not going to sit there."

He actually takes hold of my arm and pulls me down the table. He puts me between him and Raoul—as far away as possible from the Crown Prince, my father, and of course Christophe.

The Crown Prince and the rest of the Royal Family stand and watch from their end of the table. None of them intervenes until Remi pushes me into a random chair and parks himself next to me.

Raoul obviously wasn't expecting this, but he sits down on my other side anyway.

The place card in front of me says, *Marcel Lefebvre,* on it. Marcel sits in my old place between Simone and Emeline.

No one makes any comment about him posing a threat to them or them posing a threat to him.

The rest of both families sit down. The hostility and explosive energy pulses through the room at an epic pitch, but no one acts on it.

The Crown Prince waves my father to the chair at the Prince Gustav's right hand. Christophe sits on his father's other side.

The servers start going around the room pouring drinks and passing out hors d'oeuvres to everyone. A few people start talking to each other on either side or across the table.

Marcel starts talking to both Simone and Emeline like his family and theirs never disliked each other at all. Emeline laughs at something he says.

The Crown Prince, my father, and Christophe start talking, too, but I can't hear them over the general hubbub in the room. The clink of silverware and all the other voices drown out their conversation, but I already know what they're talking about.

"They can't seriously expect to just marry you off for political gain," Remi mutters under his breath.

"Why can't they?" I ask. "The Royal Houses of Europe have been doing the same thing for centuries—maybe even millennia. They can do the same thing now."

"This is the twenty-first century!" he hisses. "It's barbaric! Just look at them. The Prince's oldest son is in hiding and wanted on criminal charges. His father disowned him and the Royal Family disavowed him. No one even knows where he is in spite of the authorities scouring the world for him." He snorts at the Royal Family. "I'll bet every single one of them is as rotten as he is."

"Maybe everyone is sick and tired of this feud going on between our families," I tell him. "Maybe it's time to put it to rest—and what better way than for Silvain Lefebvre's daughter to marry the Crown Prince's son? It sounds like a fairy tale."

"It sounds like a nightmare!" he snaps. "Don't tell me you actually want to marry him."

"I didn't say I was happy about it. He looks like the biggest shark in the pond."

Remi snorts again. Raoul overhears our conversation and chimes in, but he doesn't turn his head. He faces straight in front of him so he doesn't draw attention to himself. "We might be able to turn this to our advantage."

"How?!" Remi snaps. "How does selling our sister to our worst enemy help us at all? We should be arming for war—not making peace with them."

"We are arming for war, brother," Raoul murmurs. "We're sending a spy behind enemy lines to strike the enemy where it hurts."

Remi's head shoots up. "What?"

Raoul finally turns his head and looks down into my eyes. "You'll be closer to Christophe than anyone. He's the Prince's heir. You'll be able to hit him where it counts and strike a blow against the Prince."

I glance down the table toward Christophe. I'm just in the middle of saying, "I don't know about that......" when he happens to look up at me. He only makes eye contact for a split second before he looks away.

That moment sends a shiver up my spine. I don't know anything about him, but he isn't the kind that will be easily duped into anything. He understands this agreement as well as I do—maybe even better than I do.

His brothers and cousins don't talk much on their side of the table—or if they do, they talk to their sisters, aunt, and female cousins.

I only have to look around me to see them all planning the same thing. The Royal Family is treating this as an act of war, too.

This arranged marriage between me and Christophe that my father and the Crown Prince are planning right now—this won't bring peace to our families—not at all.

"This is a really terrible idea," I murmur under my breath.

"I've been saying that from the beginning," Remi snaps.

"It's a great idea," Raoul repeats. "We should have thought of this a long time ago, but I suppose you weren't old enough to get married. That's okay. We'll just have to make the most of it now while we have the chance."

Almost at his word, the Crown Prince stands up. That's the signal for everyone else to do the same thing even though the servers haven't started serving the meal yet.

The Crown Prince and my father stroll out of the dining room side by side like they're the best of friends. Christophe follows and stays with them.

The rest of the group trails out behind those three. I would be getting lost in the shuffle, but Raoul and Remi never leave me alone for an instant. They flank me in a guarding posture to keep everyone in the Royal Family away from me, including the women.

Pascal happens to get too close to me, but anyone can see it's completely unintentional. He's the Crown Prince's third son, younger than Christophe and older than Renáld.

No one considers Pascal a threat. He was born with his face badly deformed. He's hideously ugly and always keeps to himself. He never gives interviews, never leaves the palace unless he's going somewhere with his family, and never speaks in public.

No one knows anything about his personality. Maybe he doesn't even have one. Everyone prefers to forget he exists.

Remi and Raoul sure treat him as a threat. They cut between him and me, nudge him out of the way, and give him threatening looks to make him back off.

He immediately looks away from them and doesn't say a word even to apologize before he retreats to the other side of the group.

I really wish Remi and Raoul would stop acting this way, but it doesn't really make any difference in the end.

I've been expressing my doubts about this arranged marriage ever since my father first came up with the idea. No one will listen.

My two older sisters and all my other relatives think it's high time the Lefebvre family made peace with the Royal Family of Monaco. No one can even remember how the feud started.

I never wanted to go through with an arranged marriage in the first place, but my brothers' comments make this sound like an even worse idea than it already was.

This is bound to end badly—and I'll be the one caught in the middle of it.

Chapter 2: Christophe

"You aren't really going to go through with this, are you?" my cousin Casim snaps.

"I agree with Casim," Salvatore adds. "This is a terrible idea. How do we know this isn't a trick by the Lefebvre family to stab the Crown Prince in the back?"

"Try to explain that to Father," I reply over my shoulder while I straighten my vest, tie, and shirt cuffs. "If you can convince him, more power to you."

"You better protect yourself from her," my other cousin Dorian points out. "They could be trying to slip her inside your room to kill you or something."

I snort at him. "She's half my size. I think I can handle her."

"I'm not so sure about that," Pascal chimes in. "Did you see the way she was looking around the table at dinner the other night? She looked as anxious about this as we are. She doesn't want to go through with this any more than we do. Her father is making her do it."

"I saw the same thing and I agree with you," I tell him. "Did you see her brothers talking to her? They're the ones we have to worry about."

"You're deluding yourself," Dorian counters. "She's one of them. She wouldn't betray her own family—not for us, not for the Royal House, and certainly not for you. If you saw all that, then you must have seen her glaring at you. She hates you."

I try to laugh that off. "Then we're even because I hate her, too." I turn around and start pulling on my jacket. "Don't worry. I'll keep an eye on her. Besides, I'm about to be alone with her in a closed room. If she plans to try anything, she should show it now."

"Give her a chance, Christophe," Pascal tells me. "Don't automatically assume she's hostile or dangerous. Let her show herself before you make up your mind."

"I plan to, brother. Now please stop talking about this. I have to go."

I straighten my jacket and adjust my appearance one last time before I walk out of the room. My brothers and cousins come with me.

We leave the drawing room where I've been getting ready, pass down the long, wide, ornately tiled palace corridors, and enter a different drawing room right outside the grand palace ballroom.

Silvain Lefebvre and his family are already in there, including Silvain's sons, Raoul, Remi, and Marcel, plus Silvain's nephews, Gabriel and René.

My gaze snaps to Geneviève. She's wearing a much simpler dress this time than the one she wore to the formal arrangement dinner. This one is a knee-length, green business dress with a band around the waist and a beige blazer over it.

She has a nice body. I have to give her that much. She's a very well taken care of young lady of twenty-three.

She isn't bad looking, either. She wore her chestnut hair flowing out across her pale shoulders the night of the dinner. It sets off her green eyes and dainty lips.

Now she wears her hair twisted up in a tasteful swooping ridge up the back of her head. She would look attractive either way if she wasn't my family's worst enemy.

Her eyes go cold and her walls come up when she sees me looking at her. No one has to explain any of this to her—or me.

I find myself studying her while my father and Silvain go through the usual pleasantries. I don't need to listen to any of that.

The two of them have already decided to go through with this arranged marriage. That's one thing you learn quickly when you grow up in the Royal Family. Never question Father's decisions.

He's the Crown Prince. What he says goes. Arguing about it won't make any difference except perhaps to make it worse for the person arguing against it.

Silvain Lefebvre's daughter is the absolute last person on Planet Earth I would ever marry. I can't think of any good reason to bring a viper like that into the Royal Palace, but my father didn't ask for my opinion.

He's doing this for the good of the monarchy. That's the only explanation. He thinks the feud between the Royal Family and the Lefebvre family is hurting the monarchy somehow.

Just don't ask me how it's hurting us. I don't see that it effects the Royal Family at all, but I'm not the Crown Prince—not yet.

I guess I'll just be one of those princes who keeps a mistress on the side. I'll find the girl I really want to spend my time with. I'll make public appearances with Geneviève and then I'll just live a shadow life behind the scenes.

I wouldn't be the first man to do it and I'm sure I won't be the last.

It isn't the way I want to live, though. I was raised to be a faithful father and husband to one woman—ideally the woman who would become my Crown Princess after my father dies.

It twists the knife in my guts that the title will go to one of our enemies. I'll never be able to trust her, but I guess all of that is someone else's decision, too.

My father waves me forward. Geneviève tells me it's nice to see me again and holds out her hand. I kiss the back of her knuckles and tell her the pleasure is all mine.

These formalities mean exactly nothing. Our mouths say one thing while we're both thinking the opposite.

My father and Silvain exchange a few more meaningless pleasantries before my father says, "Let's take a walk around the palace and leave these two to get to know each other better."

I stay where I am and wait for everyone else to leave. At least Geneviève and I won't have to make conversation while everyone stands around listening to every word.

Heaven knows we'll get scrutinized by the press every time we step outside. Everyone will examine our relationship under a microscope in search of any sign that it isn't real.

We'll have to get very good at acting and pretending that we're deeply in love. I don't look forward to that, but I'll do it for the monarchy and the family.

I wait just long enough for the door to close behind Marcel. Then I throw myself down on the nearest couch and prop my foot on the table in front of me.

"Take a seat," I tell her. "There's no need to be so formal."

She doesn't move. Her expression turns to granite—even more than it was before. "No, thank you," she simpers. "I'll stand."

My head shoots up and I stare at her. "You don't have to like it any better than I do. You might as well sit down and make yourself comfortable until they come back."

She still doesn't move. She stares off in another direction.

I can't believe what I'm seeing. Does she really plan to just ignore me and give me the silent treatment—possibly forever?

I decide to try a different approach to break the ice. "When did you graduate from university? You specialized in chemistry, didn't you?"

She turns her head very slightly farther away. "I haven't graduated yet."

"Do you have another year to go? I thought you were in your third year, but I suppose I must have been mistaken."

"I was in my third year."

My ears prick up. "What do you mean—you were? Did you finish your third year, Then you have one more year, don't you?"

Her iron veneer cracks just a little bit and she looks down at her hands. "I finished my third year. My father told me not to go back."

My mouth goes dry. "Why did he do that?" I'm not sure I want to hear the answer to this.

"He told me not to go back because of this marriage arrangement," she blurts out. "He said it wouldn't do any good anyway—and he's right. It isn't as though I would ever be able to use my degree here."

I gape at the side of her face. She lets her guard down just for a second—just long enough for me to see how unbelievably devastated she is by this decision.

Jesus Christ! If I ever thought Silvain Lefebvre was a scumbag, I get the confirmation when I see what he's doing to his own daughter.

Does my father know about this? Does he have a clue that Silvain is making his daughter quit school so he can finalize this marriage?

My father would never go along with that if he knew. I'm certain of it. He would delay the marriage by at least a year—at least until she finishes her degree. That's the only decent thing to do.

He won't do it because he doesn't know about it. I can't even tell him. Silvain and Geneviève would be publicly humiliated if my father delayed or backed out on the arrangement now.

I lower my voice. I hope I sound soft enough to make her realize that I know what this means. "I'm sorry," I tell her. "I never would have agreed to this if I had known."

Her head whips around fast. "I don't need your pity!" she snaps. "This is an arrangement—nothing else. Don't you dare even think it could be anything else. Do you think I give a damn what you want or whether you're sorry? Don't try to be nice to me. Don't talk to me. Don't even look at me. I never asked for this. Don't think you're going to swoop in and save the day with your Prince Charming act. Just leave me alone and I'll leave you alone. Don't make it worse than it is by trying to sugar-coat it into something else."

She immediately looks away, but those words switch my mind off. What a heartless, unfeeling witch.

I snort again and stand up, but I don't walk away. This is my house—not hers. I walk right up next to her so she'll be certain to hear every word I say. I bend in low next to her face even though she's still facing away from me.

"Don't worry," I hiss. "That is the last time I will ever try to be nice to you. You want to be alone? That's exactly what you'll get."

I turn away and walk out of the room. I make sure to walk out calmly and I leave the doors standing wide open. My father and hers will come back and find her alone.

Heartless witch. Never again. She can take care of herself for all I care.

She's a statue in the corner as far as I'm concerned. She's nothing. She's a piece of furniture. That's all she's good for.

Chapter 3: Geneviève

My two older sisters Marina and Cécile hover around me straightening my wedding veil. "You look beautiful," Marina breathes and blinks tears out of her eyes.

Fortunately, the veil hides her agonized features. I pretend to look in the mirror behind her, but I'm really just staring into space waiting for the moment of truth. I don't want anyone being happy about this wedding.

I'll go downstairs in a minute, get into a limo, and ride to the cathedral to marry Christophe. I'll go through all of that while the press films and photographs the whole royal wedding.

Women and girls all over Europe will sob into their handkerchiefs and tissues because Christophe won't be on the market anymore. No one will be able to call him the most eligible bachelor in Europe anymore.

I'm sure that won't stop him from getting any girl he wants. The press doesn't say anything about him playing around, but he could if he wanted to.

He'll probably go all out and enjoy himself, now that he's safely married. No one will expect him to do anything responsible with women ever again because he'll already be taken—in name at least.

I don't know why I'm even thinking this—except that I always secretly hoped I would find love and happiness with someone.

That will never happen now. What a mockery this wedding is turning into. It's the opposite of everything a wedding should be.

I sigh and give it up. I've been going around and around in my mind all this time about whether I should go through with this.

It's the morning of the wedding, so it's too late for me to back out now. I'm already wearing my dress and waiting for the limo to come and pick me up.

My aunt Aline comes into the room. "The limo is here, darling." She steps in front of me, cuts off my view of the mirror, and kisses me on the cheek. "I'm so happy for you. I know you're going to make the whole family proud."

I mumble something like, "Thank you, Auntie." I have to go.

Don't ask me why all these people are acting like I'm really marrying Christophe. I can't stand him. I hate him as much for being the guy on the other end as for being a member of the Royal Family.

That private conversation we had—the one where we were supposed to get to know each other better—that sealed the deal. Now I hate him even more.

Now he represents everything I hate about this deal. He's the reason I had to quit school. He's the reason I have to marry someone I don't like or even know.

He had to rub it in my face that I had to quit school. It isn't even that I wanted so badly to be a chemist. Some part of me always knew I wouldn't be.

I did want to get my degree, though. Now I can't even do that—because of him.

I hate him for trying to smooth it over and make it okay when it never can be. I hate him for realizing how upset I am about it.

Now I'll see all of those things every time I look at him. I wish I could slap that look right off his face, but I can't even do that.

I lift my skirts to head down the sweeping hotel stairs to the lobby. Reporters pack the place on both sides.

A blinding sea of flashes and glaring lights follows me outside. Everyone snaps pictures and runs their video cameras to film me getting into the limo.

My attendants and servants follow me and carry the train of my dress. The chauffeur opens the limo door for me to get in. Then all the attendants and servants stuff the rest of the train inside with me.

Marina and Cécile get into the limo with me to ride to the church. My father, Raoul, Remi, and Marcel are already sitting in the seat inside the car, so we definitely can't talk about anything now.

My father clasps my hand. "You look stunning, my dear."

I let him kiss me on the cheek, too. At least the veil is there to stop him from touching my skin.

I shrink farther and farther away from the human race as the car glides away from the curb. I look out the window feeling.....nothing. I'm not really here. I don't exist.

The press photographs and films someone else—someone I don't know and have never heard of.

Christophe will marry some unknown, nameless, faceless, cardboard cut-out princess. He'll keep doing his thing and living his royal life over there on the other side of the country.

I'll keep living my normal life and doing my thing. I'll keep living so far away from him that I'm barely aware of his existence. I'll hear about him and his new bride in the press. Other than that, he might as well be on the moon.

The limo stops in front of the cathedral. I see myself from a million miles away. I could be watching this happen in a dream for all I care.

My father kisses me again, congratulates me, and gets out of the car with my sisters and my aunt. Then Marcel gets out.

My sisters and the attendants gather around the car waiting for me to get out so they can help me with my skirts and train.

I'm just about to heave myself outside when Raoul stops me. He grabs my arm, pulls me back inside, and shoves something into my hand.

"Take this," he whispers. "Don't let anyone see it."

I look down at a gun in my hand. It's a small revolver barely big enough to fit in my palm.

I blink at it in disbelief. Is this real?

"As soon as you get into Christophe's apartment, you can shoot him and escape through the patio doors," Raoul goes on in a hushed murmur. "That will lead you out into the grounds. You can escape from the palace that way."

"As soon as you leave the apartment, turn left off the balcony, throw the gun into the bushes, follow the pathway past the rose garden, and step up onto the bench against the wall," Remi tells me. "We'll station our men there to meet you and drive you away from the palace. Don't worry about anything. We'll make sure nothing happens to you afterward. We'll send you into hiding until this whole thing blows over."

I can't stop staring at the gun. They want me to shoot Christophe? Seriously?

My father startles me back to my senses by calling from outside the car. "Darling! It's time to go!"

"I can't do this!" I shove the gun back toward Raoul. "I can't! It isn't right!"

"You have to!" He pushes my hand back at me. "Hide the gun in your clothes so you have it with you when you leave the cathedral to go back to the palace. Understand? Wait until you're alone with him and he lets his guard down. Shoot him while he's asleep if you have to."

My father bends down and calls through the door just then. "What's taking so long?"

I lower my hand to the seat to hide the gun. I can't wait any longer.

I use that hand to scoop up my skirts. The billowing layers cover the gun and hide it from view.

I don't want to take a gun into the cathedral when I'm supposed to be getting married. I can't believe I'm actually holding a gun that I'm supposed to use to kill Christophe—the groom I'm about to marry.

This is a nightmare, but my nightmare becomes complete when my sisters lead me into the rectory next to the church entrance.

They start arranging and straightening my skirts and veil that may have gotten crumpled on the trip over here.

I take that moment to turn my back on my sisters and stuff the gun into my bra. It's the only place I have left to hide it, but my tight bodice won't let me hide it there. Everyone would be able to see it.

I make an excuse that I have to go to the bathroom. I hide the gun under my skirts again. I have to gather them up in both arms and wedge myself into the bathroom.

My sisters stand outside and wait for me to finish and wash my hands. I take a split second after I pull up my underwear to stash the gun in my garter belt.

The garter belt is supposed to be the bride's sexy little secret. The groom is supposed to throw her garter belt to the single male wedding guests right after she throws her bouquet.

We definitely won't be doing that at this wedding. I would never let Christophe get close enough to me even to see my garter belt, much less take it off.

The gun burns a hole in my skin and balances there against my thigh. The gun demands all my attention when I go back out into the main rectory room and finish getting ready for the ceremony.

My full skirts hide the gun from everyone but me. This wedding is turning into something more like a horror movie.

My father comes back and tells me it's time. My sisters leave first. I guess they're going through the procession of family members entering the church and taking their places near the altar.

My father takes my hand and places it on his arm. This would be one of the most meaningful moments of our relationship, but instead, it's turning into one of the most horrific.

He's the one doing this to me. He's giving me in marriage to his worst enemy—and for what? What do he and Crown Prince Gustav stand to gain by this marriage? I really don't have any answer for that.

If anything, this marriage seems to be escalating hostilities between our families instead of lessening them.

Chapter 4: Christophe

I stand in a little antechamber outside the church while we wait for Geneviève and her family to show up in the limo.

I obsessively adjust and readjust my tux while I wait. Maybe Geneviève will get cold feet and back out before the actual wedding. That will let me off the hook and I won't have to go through with it, either.

My brothers and cousins move around the room pretending to stay busy, but there's nothing to do but wait.

I'm just about to snap my last nerve when Dorian bursts into the room. He comes straight toward me. "Here. I brought you this. Put it on under your tux."

I look down at a Kevlar bulletproof vest in his hand. "Are you insane? I'm wearing a tailored suit. I can't put that on."

He shoves the vest at me. "Put it on—now, Christophe! This could be your last chance. If the Lefebvres are going to try something, they'll do it now before you can bring in anyone to stop them. You're going to be alone with one of them for a long time from now on. Now put it on and don't make me tell you again."

I don't argue any further. I take the vest and get busy stripping off my jacket, vest, shirt, and tie that I just spent so much time putting on.

"We have security all over the cathedral," Dorian goes on. "They'll be flanking you all the way back to the palace, but we can't put security inside the car with you and Geneviève on your way back to the palace."

"And we won't be able to station security inside your bedroom, either," Casim adds. "Be extra careful there."

I snort at him. "Don't you think you're taking this a little too far? This isn't the Middle Ages, you know. She isn't going to try to kill me."

"It never hurts to take precautions. You want to be prepared if she does try something."

"When and how would she try something? She won't have a weapon with her in the church. Where would she hide it?"

"In her bra," Salvatore suggests.

"In her underwear," Casim adds.

I burst out laughing. "That would corrode the metal."

They snort with laughter, but just then, the priest sticks his head in. "The bride's limo is just arriving now. You might want to come outside."

I finish strapping the Velcro around my chest. I wear a grey T-shirt under my shirt, so I put the vest outside the T-shirt and under my dress shirt.

I'm just about to put my shirt back on when Dorian comes over to me, rips out all the Velcro straps, and tightens them. "This will keep you alive," he tells me. "It needs to be tight."

I don't argue while he manhandles me. He cinches the straps so tight that I can hardly breathe. He jerks me back and forth, slaps the vest, grabs it by the arm holes, and yanks it to make sure it's tight enough.

He furrows his brow and glares at both me and the vest while he does it. I don't argue. I know him better than to think he's mad at me. He's furious that I'm even in this situation.

At least my brothers and cousins care enough to try to protect me. I would be stupid to argue with that.

I'm usually working with them to deal with threats to the Royal Family's security. Now I'm the object of that threat.

He finally slaps me on the sternum. "Put your clothes on, man. You're ready."

A tense silence falls over the group when I start pulling my shirt on. They all stand around watching me button my shirt over the vest and then put on the vest and the jacket.

I straighten my clothes in front of the mirror for the second time. The tux hides the extra thickness of the bulletproof vest under my suit. No one will be able to tell.

I actually feel better, now that I'm wearing it. I might still get shot, but at least I won't get shot in the chest.

I could still die from a gunshot wound to the head if Geneviève really is out to kill me.

I put those thoughts out of my head. I really need to listen to Pascal. He's a lot smarter than anyone gives him credit for. Everyone is too distracted by how ugly he is.

He saw a lot more in Geneviève than anyone else at that dinner. She doesn't want to do this. Her father and brothers are putting her up to it.

They'll be the ones putting her up to killing me, too—if she's going to try to kill me at all. She isn't coming up with this on her own.

She didn't come up with the idea to infiltrate our family so she could kill me. She definitely didn't volunteer to marry me so she could carry out a hit like this on the Royal Family.

I have to remember that. I have to remember that she's a pawn in the game. I might even be able to consider her a victim.

I still have to take precautions, though—and now I am. I'm wearing a bulletproof vest to my own wedding. If that isn't taking precautions, I don't know what is.

The priest comes back, tells us again that we really need to get to the altar, and my brothers and cousins surround me on our way out of the room.

I take my place at the altar. Pascal and Renáld stand behind me. Dorian, Casim, and Salvatore stand behind them in a line.

All five of them will tackle me, protect me with their bodies, and drag me out of the cathedral to a waiting car out back if anything goes wrong. I don't have to worry about that, but I wind up worrying about it anyway.

Tradition calls for me to stand with my back to the pews and wait for Geneviève to join me. I'm not supposed to turn around or see her until she stops next to me.

I concentrate on the statues surrounding the altar and on the wall behind it. Candles flickers and incense smokes around the giant crucifix hanging on the back wall.

The carved statue of Jesus stares straight down at me. Should I take any meaning from that stare? Is he trying to tell me something?

I let my thoughts run away with me. I don't notice anything else until someone stops at my side. I glance down and see Geneviève in her wedding dress and veil.

She looks pretty until she looks up at me. The expression of abject horror in her eyes makes me immediately look away. Damn, she really doesn't want to do this.

I face front and barely pay enough attention to the service to hear when the priest tells us to kneel or stand.

I go through everything in a dull trance. It doesn't mean a thing. I might as well be standing here enduring a tedious state parade or some other event. I've been attending them all my life. I'm used to the boredom by now.

Only part of me even remembers that I'm wearing a bulletproof vest. Is Geneviève going to pull an assault rifle from under her dress and open fire right here in the church?

That's ridiculous because she couldn't hide an assault rifle under that tight dress—but what about a handgun?

She would be able to hide it under her wide, billowing skirts. She could hide a whole arsenal of handguns under there.

My mind spins off in some strange directions. Maybe getting married does this to everyone.

I'm not about to assign one of my brothers or security guys the task of searching under some woman's dress for hidden handguns. Dorian might think that's a good idea, but I'm not that far gone.

The priest tells Geneviève and me to kneel again. He goes through the entire Mass and gives us both communion. Then he gets to the vows.

I say, "I do," at the appropriate place and so does Geneviève. She doesn't pull out any guns or open fire. She could definitely kill me first if she did.

The priest eventually states that the service is at an end, instructs the congregation to go in peace and all that, and the organ starts playing again.

Geneviève and I both get to our feet and turn around. We come face to face, but she only looks more petrified.

That's what this is. She isn't horrified by the idea of marrying me because she hates me so much. She's scared out of her wits.

Seeing that makes me want to help her. I might not be able to and I'm certain she doesn't want me to, but I want to. I wish she didn't have to go through with this—but it looks like she already did. We're married.

I offer her my arm and she takes it. Then we both face the crowd of reporters blocking our way out of the building.

I do my best to smile. I don't look to see if Geneviève is smiling. A million flash bulbs blind me from seeing anything anyway.

The palace security team eventually moves in and signals us to move down the aisle. The reports fall back flashing just as many pictures in our faces.

The security team forms a ring around me and Geneviève. She still doesn't pull a gun. Is she waiting until she gets outside?

We have to stop on the church steps, smile some more, and wave to the crowds of civilians packed behind Police barricades. The army of reporters fills the whole street.

Geneviève and I stand there smiling and waving at everyone for another eternity. I lose track of time until a limo pulls up in front of us.

Two flanks of Police have to work their way into the press corps and force everyone out of the way so the limo can get through.

Geneviève and I get in along with five security guys from the palace team.

Geneviève sits on the opposite seat. She doesn't look at me even once on the way to the reception. It's being held at one of the biggest hotels in Monte Carlo. I don't know any of the other details. That's someone else's department.

The security team doesn't give me or Geneviève a chance to say anything on the way there. They hustle us out of the car and into the hotel before anyone else arrives.

The team takes us into a private room off the hall where the reception will be held. This would probably be the time when Geneviève and I would be able to spend some time alone together before the reception kicks off into high gear.

The security team doesn't leave us alone. The guys keep talking to me about all the precautions they're taking. Some of them speak into their earpieces or into handheld radios to coordinate with the rest of the team, including my brothers and cousins.

Geneviève gets isolated on the other side of the room. I try to go over there to stand next to her, but the security guys keep cutting me off.

She cowers away from them. She looks more terrified and agitated here than she did at the church.

The idea of going out and facing all those people must be putting her on edge. I sure wish she would let me put her at ease, but she doesn't want that, either.

I don't get a chance to go near her before my brothers and cousins show up. Renáld and Dorian come right up to me.

Dorian gives me a hard look. "You okay?"

I nod. "Fine. You saw the ceremony. It went without a hitch."

"The reception better go the same way," he growls.

"Our guys will circulate in the crowd," Renáld tells me. "The Lefebvres have their own people coming to the reception, too, so we'll have some of our guys stationed near you at all times. They'll be keeping an eye on things, especially when one of the Lefebvres comes over to talk to you. Be ready in case something happens."

I glance over at Geneviève again, but she's too far away and there's too much noise in here. She can't hear our conversation.

I cringe when I think about treating her family as murderous enemies, but it only takes one bad apple to prove my brothers and cousins right. If even one of the Lefebvres is planning anything, we have to keep an eye on all of them.

I don't want to include Geneviève in that, but she is a Lefebvre. That's the whole point of this.

The time comes for everyone to go out to the reception. The guests are all here. My brothers and cousins leave first so they can go mill around in the crowd like regular guests.

The security team surrounds me and Geneviève. She takes my arm as we leave the room together.

Cheers erupt when we walk into the hall. More press flashes and yells flood the hall—and then it's all on.

Geneviève stands with her hand on my arm while dozens of people come past to congratulate us. I turn my brain off, shake their hands, and thank them. Their faces blur together. I don't see or hear anything else except for Geneviève doing the same thing.

She talks in a soft, smooth voice. She sounds kind. I'm the one she really hates and now she'll never get rid of me.

Chapter 5: Geneviève

The Royal Family's security team surrounds me and forms a protective barricade so I can run to the limo outside the hotel. The reception is over.

Now I'm supposed to go home with Christophe. I'm going home to the Royal Palace, which is where I'm supposed to live from now on.

I still don't let myself believe I'm married to him. This can't be real—but it is. I went through the ceremony. I went through the vows. I even went through the reception, the wedding meal, cutting the cake, and everything else.

I sit down in the limo and Christophe climbs in after me. I scoot down the seat to make room for the security guys to get in.

The door slams and the car starts moving. I look around in panic when I realize there are no security guys in here with us. I'm alone with Christophe in a car moving down the street toward the palace.

He collapses back on the seat and lets out a gasp of exasperation and relief. "Thank God that's over! I thought it would never end."

I glance in his direction. It really is him. I've been standing next to him all day, but I never really had to face him or look him in the eye.

I tricked myself into believing that none of this was real. Now I'm stuck in this car with him—and that's nothing compared to what will happen when we get back to the palace.

I try to look away. I can't make eye contact with him. I'm still carrying around this gun under my skirts. What am I going to do with it?

I can't shoot him. I could never shoot any living human being. I don't care how much I hate him or his family.

I freeze to my seat when he sits up, leans forward, and starts stripping off his jacket. He tears off his vest, unbuttons his shirt, and I stare in mute horror when I see that he's wearing a bulletproof vest under his tux.

He starts ripping off the Velcro straps, yanks the vest off, and throws it on the seat next to him with another growl of exasperation. "I guess I don't need that anymore."

I look back and forth between him and the vest. He wore a bulletproof vest to the wedding. Did he know I was going to bring a gun? How could he know when Raoul only gave me the gun a few minutes before the ceremony?

No one from my family would have told anyone from the Royal Family that Raoul gave me the gun. No one from my family would have had time to tell anyone in the Royal Family or Christophe's security team.

He flops back onto the seat wearing nothing but a grey T-shirt underneath. He laughs when he sees me sitting there with my mouth open. "You weren't really going to shoot me, were you?"

"I....I didn't.....I mean....." I struggle to come up with something to say—something other than the truth.

He looks out the window at the scenery passing. "You can't blame my family for taking precautions. My father might not want to believe

Silvain could come up with all of this as an elaborate murder plot to get someone from your family inside our house." He glances at me once and looks away. "Don't worry. It's just the usual paranoia getting the better of certain people. I know you weren't really going to shoot me."

I open and close my mouth a few times, but I can't make a sound. I'm done for if he finds out about the gun—or if anyone else from his family or the palace security team finds out. I can't let that happen.

I can't believe I let Raoul talk me into this. My mind races for a way to get rid of the gun before someone sees it or finds it.

I won't be able to hide it in the palace. Any of the servants might stumble upon it.

I don't even know my way around the Royal Palace. How am I supposed to find a place to hide a gun—somewhere no one will ever find it?

He laughs again when he sees me in so much distress. "Maybe I should wear the vest on our wedding night. If you really wanted to kill me, all you have to do is cut off my erection. I'll bleed to death—or you can slit my throat while I sleep. The vest wouldn't help me then."

All the blood drains from my cheeks and head. I can't think. Does he really think I would go that far to kill him?

I can't stand the way he's looking at me. I tear my eyes away and wind up looking out the window.

"Don't worry. I was only joking," he tells me from behind. "I was trying to lighten the mood. I didn't mean to scare you."

I can't look at him or talk to him. He thinks it's a joke that I would try to kill him. What will he do when he finds out Raoul really did set me up to shoot Christophe?

The security team will arrest me. I might even get the death penalty or life in prison. I don't even know the laws of Monaco well enough to know how bad it could get.

Christophe trying to be lighthearted about it only makes this so much worse. I could kick Raoul for putting me in this situation. Now I have to find a way to get out of it.

The limo pulls inside the palace gates and drives around to a covered archway in the back. The security team meets us there, but they don't accompany Christophe and me inside.

He puts his arm behind my back like he really is my husband or something. I'm too out of my mind with agitation to decide what to do about it.

We pass through a narrow, unassuming door and enter a long corridor. It leads to another door that opens into one of the palace's grand, high-ceilinged passageways leading to the sweeping staircase.

Christophe shows me into a different wing of the palace. I've never been here before—and I find out why when he opens a door somewhere and escorts me inside.

We walk into a giant apartment with its own luxurious living room, a courtyard leading into the garden and grounds, multiple bedrooms off the living room, and a huge, stately bathroom.

Christophe stops trying to escort me around the minute we walk through the door. "Make yourself at home," he tells me. "Your luggage is in that bedroom over there."

He points to a giant bedroom on the left. Huge French doors let sunshine stream over the magnificent bed. The doors lead onto another patio that connects up with the palace grounds.

I can't think about anything other than getting as far away from Christophe as possible—and getting the gun as far away from Christophe as possible.

He makes it easier for me by throwing his jacket across the couch and flopping down on the cushions like he's exhausted. He pretends not to see me go into the other bedroom and shut the door behind me.

I get busy taking off my wedding dress and veil. Now I have no choice but to deal with the gun tucked into my garter.

I take the gun out and throw it on the bedspread while I think it over. Should I put the gun under the mattress—or flush it down the toilet?

It won't flush down the toilet. That will only clog the toilet and draw more attention to whatever is clogging it.

I take my regular clothes out of the suitcase while I think about it—or struggle to think about it. I could put the gun between the rolled-up towels in the bathroom—but then the maids would find the gun when they clean this room.

I come to a halt there in the middle room, turn in a complete circle, and take in the whole scene. This is one of the nicest rooms I've ever seen with its big, fancy, luxurious bathroom and sun-washed patio outside.

This room is my prison now. I have to find some way to hide the gun in here, but even that won't solve my problem.

In the end, I'll still have to find a way to get rid of the gun entirely. I really need to find a way to destroy it—but how?

I can't risk Christophe, anyone in his family, or any of his security people finding the gun. I can't even let them find out about the gun.

They'll only come to one conclusion if they do find out about it. They'll realize I brought the gun here to kill Christophe.

I didn't bring it here to kill Christophe. I never wanted to bring the gun at all.

I realize too late that I shouldn't have brought the gun here at all. I should have sent my sisters and my cousin out of the rectory room and hidden the gun there. That would have been the smarter way to handle it.

Now I'm stuck with it.

I get progressively more agitated the longer I stand here thinking about it. I have to do something—but I can't think of anything to do.

I can't see any place in this room or the bathroom that Christophe will absolutely never look. The only place I can think of is my own suitcase.

As soon as I think that, I make up my mind and attack the suitcase in a frenzy. I haul it onto the bed and wrap the gun in a bunch of my underwear. Christophe won't look at that—or maybe he will. Maybe he's a closet pervert and I don't even know how perverted he can be.

This is only temporary. I'm only putting the gun here until I can find a more permanent way to get rid of it. This is the best I can do for now.

Maybe something will happen. Maybe my family will come over to the palace to have dinner with the Royal Family, now that we're all best friends.

Then I'll be able to return the gun to Raoul—but that might cause Raoul to use the gun to try to kill Christophe.

I cover my face and force myself to breathe. This is a nightmare. How did I ever get myself into this?

I come out of the bedroom as casually as I can. Christophe is still sitting there on the couch looking at his phone. He props one foot on the coffee table in front of him and doesn't look up when I come out.

He waves over his shoulder. "You can call down to the kitchens and let them know if you want to eat anything tonight. I don't know what you like or if you're still too stuffed from the reception, but help yourself."

I choose my next words with care. "What do you want to do about tonight?"

He keeps looking down at his phone, but his eyes snap away from the screen when he realizes what I mean.

He recovers instantly and goes back to tapping on the screen. "I don't care what we do tonight. I'll stay in that room over there."

"What about.......?" I can't say it.

According to tradition and the law, we aren't legally married until we consummate it.

He only slouches sideways on the couch still keeping his face glued to his phone. "I don't care about that. This is just an arrangement like you said. You stay over there and I'll stay over there. We don't have to bother each other."

"You.....you don't want to?"

He snorts, looks up at me once, and goes straight back to what he was doing. "I don't want any of this any more than you do, honey. You do your own thing and I'll do mine."

He bends over the phone and puts me out of his mind. I follow his gesture and find a list of palace phone numbers. This apartment must be for guests—or it was before we started staying here.

One of the numbers is for the kitchens, but I couldn't eat anything right now to save my life. I put the list down and hunt through the apartment for no apparent reason.

I'm not looking for a hiding place for the gun anymore—not in here. Nothing in here will be hidden enough.

I'm not likely to find a kiln outside where I can melt down the gun, either. I need to come up with some other solution.

I noodle around the apartment for a while trying to distract myself. Christophe never looks up. He pretends I'm not there.

I don't need to be here if he's going to keep pretending that. Thinking about finding a kiln to melt down the gun gives me an idea.

I go into the bedroom, dig the gun out of my wad of underwear, wrap it in a washcloth from the bathroom, and stuff the gun down inside my underwear where my blouse will cover the bulge in my pants.

I look like a man, but I just have to hope no one pays too much attention. I slide open the glass doors leading to the bedroom patio. I'm all alone here. Christophe doesn't care what I do.

I slip out into the grounds and take off walking as fast as I dare down one of the lawn avenues between stately trees on one side and a maze of hedges on the other. I don't dare to run. That will definitely look suspicious.

I get to the far end of the maze and duck into the trees. I work my way all the way back from the avenue where no one will be able to see me.

I stop there and look around everywhere before I go down on my knees. I scratch, claw, dig with my fingernails, and gouge out a hole in the soft soil. I just hope the hole is deep enough.

Maybe the palace security team regularly sweeps the grounds with a metal detector in search of hidden firearms. How should I know?

I stop and hold my breath to listen before I stash the gun there. My chest hurts from breathing so heavily—not to mention the anxiety of what I'm doing.

I don't hear anything. The pounding of my heart in my ears makes it difficult to concentrate.

I fumble to pull the wad out of my pants, unwrap the washcloth, and tip the gun into the hole. I hope the moist soil corrodes the metal and eventually rots it away. Then I won't be able to use it.

I don't want to use it. I don't want to have it. I don't even want to know it exists. I'm really starting to hate Raoul and the rest of my family for putting me in this situation.

How dare they? I'm the one who will face the consequences—not any of them. They can all afford to hate the Royal Family from a safe distance while I run all the risk.

I never asked for this. It's bad enough that my father married me to Christophe for political gain. Raoul and Remi didn't have to make it worse by telling me to kill the guy into the bargain.

I bury the gun, press down the soil to make it as smooth as possible, and cover it with dry leaves. Maybe some kind of tracking expert would be able to tell that someone dug a hole here, but I can't see the difference.

That's the best I can do right now. I stuff the washcloth back into my pants and hustle back to the apartment.

I make sure to go through the bedroom patio entrance again. The bedroom door is still closed between the bedroom and the living room. Christophe can't see me.

I go into the bathroom, wash my hands, and make sure to scrape every speck of dirt out from under my fingernails.

Then I open the bedroom door to make it look less suspicious. I take my nail kit to the living room and sit across the room from Christophe to give myself a manicure.

He doesn't look up, so he doesn't see me using the manicure tools to remove every last trace of evidence that I ever messed up my nails.

Chapter 6: Christophe

The tension coming from Geneviève spikes off the charts the minute we set foot inside my apartment. She shouldn't be this nervous. The wedding is over. She should be relaxing.

Her agitation only gets worse after she changes out of her wedding dress. Something is definitely wrong with her.

I keep my head down and pay attention to my phone, but I use my ears to track her around the apartment. She isn't doing anything except trying to deflect me from seeing everything she isn't doing.

Her behavior makes me suspicious—much more suspicious than I would be otherwise. She can see I'm not interested in forcing myself on her or anything like that. She should be calming down, now that she isn't under any more pressure to perform in public.

The way she acted in the limo on the way here definitely raised my suspicions. She acted way too shocked when she saw me wearing a bulletproof vest, but that was nothing compared to the way she acted when I took the vest off.

She acted more horrified that I took it off in front of her than that I was wearing it at all. Did she really plan to harm me? Does she really?

I tried to test her by suggesting that she kill me by cutting my prick off. That might have been crude and cruel, but it worked.

A normal person would have laughed about it or reprimanded me for saying something so rude and vulgar when we were on our way home from getting married.

I hate to admit it, but she really did act like she might have been planning to do exactly that—and got caught planning it. I have to look into this.

I navigate on my phone and bring up the palace security system while she goes back into the bedroom. The room doesn't have security cameras, but I can access all the other cameras in the palace from here.

I locate the camera out in the grounds. It points toward the palace and I zero in on the apartment bedroom so I can see Geneviève moving around in there.

She bends over her suitcase, but she keeps her back to me so I can't see what she's doing. Then she goes into the bathroom.

She comes out, slides open the patio doors, and slips into the garden. She looks back inside the bedroom and in all directions before she takes off walking way too fast down the grassy avenue.

She's definitely acting guilty now. She's up to no good. I switch to a few different cameras of the perimeter around the palace walls, but I don't see anything out of the ordinary.

The usual people wander around on the street and a few tourists take pictures of the palace from the opposite sidewalks. That's nothing unusual.

I scroll back to the cameras located inside the grounds. I follow her down the avenue until she darts into the trees.

The cameras don't show me what's going on in there. I have to switch to a different camera located at the corner of the palace roof.

I see Geneviève messing around in the shadows between tree trunks, but I can't see what she's doing. She's definitely doing something underhanded in there. I'll have to find out what it is.

At least she isn't letting armed gunmen come over the walls into the garden, through the patio, and into the apartment to kill me that way.

I wait until she steps out onto the avenue again. She looks both ways and in all directions to make sure no one sees her. She doesn't know enough about the palace to know where all the cameras are.

She hurries back to the patio, lets herself into the bedroom, and goes to the bathroom to wash her hands. I wait until she returns to the living room.

She sits down in a nearby chair and starts filing her fingernails like she never did anything suspicious in her life.

I send Casim a text to get the security team to search that part of the grounds. I even send him a time stamp for the footage of her in there.

He answers back, *I knew it.*

Geneviève stands up just then and zips her nail kit closed. "I'm tired. I'm going to go to bed."

I wave toward the other bedroom without looking up. "Don't let me stop you."

She studies me for a second. I don't look up to see her expression. What is she thinking right now? Was she really planning to cut my prick off when I tried to do it with her? Is that why she's so agitated—because I'm not showing any sign of doing it with her?

I don't look up from my phone when I stand up and go around the room switching off the lights. I don't want them to keep her awake. That would be inconsiderate of me.

She's still standing there watching me when I go sit back down in the same place. I don't look up to see her reaction.

"We're married," she blurts out.

I pretend to look up like I just noticed her there. "Uh....I know we are."

She waves at nothing and glances in both directions. She doesn't look guilty or suspicious now. She's back to looking petrified. "We....we're supposed to do it."

My jaw hits the floor. Did she just say what I think she said?

"I mean...." she stammers. "Legally......we aren't legally married until....you know......"

My eyes fall out of their sockets. "You....you actually want to?"

"NO!!" she practically bellows. "I mean....I don't want to....but we have to....."

I blink at her in stupid disbelief. She's really suggesting that. She's standing there telling me we have to do it.

My mind turns a few somersaults while I try unsuccessfully to decide what to do about this.

I give it up in the end and turn back to my phone. "We don't have to. You go to sleep. I'll see you in the morning."

"No, really!" she blurts out. "Our families will never be at peace if we don't....I mean....you know....have children and everything."

I take extra long before I can bring myself to look up at her. The absolute sheer terror in her eyes stabs me in the guts when I actually see her features wrenching.

This is far worse than her father making her drop out of school. Did he tell her that—that the marriage wouldn't be legal unless I did it with her?

The fear in her eyes makes up my mind for me. "You obviously don't want to do it," I tell her. "So we won't do it. I'll sleep in the other room. It's no big deal. We'll just live apart. You said it was just an arrangement and that's all it is. Have a good night."

"But what about....."

I wait for her to say something else. She keeps shifting her weight from one foot to the other, knitting her fingers until her knuckles turn white, and looking everywhere but at me.

I can't stop staring at her. She really plans to go through with this even though it scares her so much.

Is this really how she plans to kill me? I can't believe that when I see how truly terrified she is. I don't believe she could go through with it even if she did plan it.

She didn't plan it—not like that. She acted too shocked when I brought it up in the limo. She may be up to something, but it isn't that.

She actually recoils and takes a step back when I stand up slowly and straighten up in front of her. Jesus, I've never seen a girl so scared! What did I ever do to make her this scared of me?

It isn't me. I never did anything to her—which means someone else made her that scared.

Was it her father—her brothers—one of her cousins? It doesn't matter because I don't plan to lay a finger on her.

Chapter 7: Christophe

Geneviève only stays in the living room for a split second before she breaks away and hurries into the bedroom in front of me. She really thinks I'm going to do it with her—as if I would ever do it with any woman who is this scared of me.

I inch over to the bedroom door and spot her standing on the opposite side of the bed—as far as she can get from me. Everything about the way she's acting hurts.

I want to leave her alone. I want to calm her down by getting as far away from her as I can, but that would probably only make her feel rejected.

Some much more powerful force is making her think she has to do this. She's more afraid of that than she is of me.

She doesn't go near the bed. She doesn't even remember to take her clothes off.

My mind goes into another tailspin thinking about how she would do all of this differently if she really planned to kill me at the moment when we consummated the marriage.

She would probably change into some revealing lingerie and stretch out on the bed all seductive and inviting. She would try to make herself irresistible to me.

She wouldn't stand over there shaking like a leaf. She's too scared even to go near the bed or pull down the covers.

Her anxiety escalates to the breaking point when I inch into the room. I have to be careful here. I can't be the one who hurts her. Someone already did that. I can't make it worse.

I really wish now that I hadn't gone through with this marriage. This was a terrible idea, but it's all done now.

I stop on my side of the bed and keep a few feet between me and the mattress. She stands over there with the bed between us.

She still won't look at me for more than a few seconds at a time. She squirms in agitation like she can't stand for me to even look at her.

"Don't worry," I murmur under my breath. "You obviously don't want this and I would never do it with someone who doesn't want to do it with me. We aren't going to do anything."

"But we have to!" she blurts out way too loudly. "If anyone found out, the marriage would be declared void and all of this....."

"Hey!" I interrupt in the same undertone. I don't want to scare her. She's scared enough already. "What about this? We'll lie on top of the mattress with our clothes on. We don't do anything. We won't even touch each other. You can get under the covers if you want to, but we won't do anything—not tonight. If we really are going to do it, we'll wait a little while—at least until we get used to each other. Okay? I'm not going to jump into bed with someone who is this scared of me. No way. I do have some honor left, you know."

Her head shoots up and she stares at me in abject shock. She's so insane with fear that I can't even tell if she heard me. She looks away just as fast.

I hold up both my hands and take one step closer to the bed. "Nice and easy....." I murmur. "No one is going to hurt you. No one is even going to touch you—not until you're ready."

I lower myself onto the mattress, prop myself on my elbow, and hold eye contact with her while I bend over and pull back the covers on her side. I leave mine tucked in.

"Get in," I tell her. "Get under the covers. I'll stay on the outside. No one is going to do anything tonight. You'll be safe in here."

She blinks down at me extra slowly. Then she looks down at the spot where the covers fold back from the sheet.

It takes her way too long to decide to do it. She moves slowly once she does, sits down, and slips her legs between the sheets.

I make a command decision not to put the covers over her. She pulls them up to her shoulder. Now she's inside the bed and I'm outside.

I bend my arm under my head and lie down on the pillow where I can see her. Her head sinks into the pillow on her side and her eyes swivel upward to me before she immediately looks away.

"So tell me why you decided to study chemistry," I tell her.

She sniffs and rolls on her back to look up at the ceiling. "I took it in high school and I really liked it. I really liked biology, especially in the advanced courses where we studied a lot of chemistry. It always interested me and I got into all the chemical interactions of microbiology and pathology. I was going to study pathology and pharmacology after I finished my undergraduate."

"You could do that now, you know."

She whips over to stare into my eyes. "What do you mean?"

My stomach turns a somersault when I see her looking deeply into my soul from inches away. She's so much more beautiful than I realized. She's beautiful on the inside—much more beautiful than she is on the outside.

I can almost imagine that we're lying here as lovers. We're talking after we just did it. She's telling me her deepest secrets.

She isn't, though. We aren't lovers. She hates me and she's scared of me. She's worried I'm going to do something awful to her.

"I mean you could study remotely and finish your degree," I tell her. "We have the internet here. You could finish your coursework and graduate the way you wanted to."

She frowns. "I don't understand. I had to give it up when I married you. I wouldn't be able to attend a university here."

"You could transfer to the International University of Monaco—or you could do it all online. You can do either one. Nothing is stopping you, now that we're actually married. You won't spend all your time attending state functions and press events. You can continue your education and go as far as you want with it."

She won't stop scowling at me. "Are you sure? Are you sure your father wouldn't object?"

"Why in God's name would he object? I'm sure he would be furious if he found out your father made you drop out of school so you could marry someone you don't know."

She looks away. "I don't want to talk about my father."

So that's it. Her father is a sore subject for her. Why am I not surprised?

"I liked biology, too," I tell her. "I didn't get to study the things I wanted to study, either—so we're in the same boat."

Her head snaps around again. "Really?"

I nod. "I wanted to study medicine—kind of like you did—but things didn't work out."

"What happened? Did your father stop you?"

"I was actually glad I wasn't the oldest son and that I wasn't going to become Crown Prince after my father died. I wanted to become a doctor and join Doctors Without Borders. I was going to travel the world doing humanitarian missions in war-torn and poverty-stricken countries. Then César got accused of murder and defrauding the Treasury. He went on the run and I had to step in as my father's heir. I had to quit medical school and dedicate myself full time to running the family business."

I smile at her to try to turn it into a joke, but she only gasps in horror again. "Oh, my God! That's awful!"

I try to shrug it off. "That's the way it goes."

"But couldn't you continue your studies remotely the way you're saying? Couldn't you at least keep exploring your own interests?"

"I did continue my studies, but I had to study political science and international affairs instead. I had to catch up on everything César had been learning up to that point. I had to get a second degree—and after that, I've been too busy to study anything."

She stares at me with a very different expression on her face. Maybe now she'll realize she isn't the only person who got thrust into a life she didn't want.

She eventually tears her gaze away. "I'm so sorry. I didn't realize that happened to you."

"Don't worry about it. I'm not telling you because I want you to feel sorry for me. I just want you to understand that I sympathize with your situation more than you probably realize. I understand what a sacrifice it was for you to quit school, but it doesn't have to stay that way. You can continue with it now. We can arrange your schedule so you have extra time away from official functions to study and maybe even attend classes—either in person or remotely."

"Wouldn't it be too complicated with security and everything if I did it in person?"

I shrug that away. "I'm sure you wouldn't have to attend in person every single time. I'm sure attending remotely would work for your everyday and weekly classes. You could attend in person if you had interviews with your advisors or if you needed to take exams or something like that. I'm in charge of palace security, so I'm sure we can work it out."

Her head shoots up again. "You are?"

I nod. Maybe I shouldn't have said that, but she doesn't get scared again.

She wilts back onto her pillow and lets out a shaky breath. "Thank you for telling me about that. I didn't know. It makes me feel better."

"Of course. Do you want to go to sleep now?"

"I guess so." She settles deeper into her pillow and shuts her eyes. Her voice starts to fade and get quieter. "Thank you for not doing it. I was really scared about doing it for the first time."

I open my mouth to tell her again that I wouldn't do it with someone who is afraid of me.

I freeze with my mouth open when I realize what she just said. "You.....you've never done it before?"

She doesn't open her eyes. Her voice starts to slur as she falls closer to the point of sleep. "I'm a virgin. I've been dreading it for a long time. It only gets worse the longer I wait. So thank you. I'm grateful."

I'm so stunned that I don't answer. I can only stare at her in stunned shock.

Her breathing rises and falls more evenly now. Her features go slack as she falls the rest of the way asleep.

She's a virgin. No wonder she was so scared about doing it. She must have built it up in her mind as this massive deal. That would throw anyone off.

Now I'm certain I can never do it with her—not as long as we're stuck in this arranged marriage. Hell no.

I settle onto my pillow to watch her sleep. I don't care if she knows the truth about me. I never wanted to be my father's heir. I only did it because I had to.

At least now she knows she isn't alone. She doesn't have to give up on her dream entirely—at least not that part of it.

She says she always knew she wasn't going to become a career chemist. Her family is too high-profile.

She definitely won't be one as the Crown Princess of Monaco. She'll have too many other duties, obligations, and responsibilities.

She can still pursue it, though. I'll always encourage her to do that.

I need to have a conversation with my father about her first. He definitely needs to know about this, but that's a conversation for tomorrow.

Chapter 8: Geneviève

I wake up alone the next day. I'm still lying in bed in the same position. I'm still wearing all the same clothes I had on when I fell asleep yesterday.

Christophe isn't here. An oblong crumpled place marks that side of the bed where he was lying when I fell asleep.

Did he stay there all night? Did we actually sleep in the same bed—or did he bail out when he realized I fell asleep on him?

I relax in bed for a while. This apartment sure is comfortable and luxurious. I don't know what else I was expecting.

I definitely wasn't expecting Christophe to be so understanding about us not doing it. Did I really think he would force it on me when I wasn't ready?

I don't know what I thought. My mind played all kinds of tricks on me about what he would want to do and what we would have to do.

Then there's the conversation we had last night. He never wanted to be his father's heir. The story about him becoming a doctor and traveling around the world doing humanitarian work—he's so different from what I thought he was.

Actually he isn't because he never became a doctor. He had to step in and take César's place. Christophe had to study politics instead.

He doesn't show any sign that he's distressed by his situation. I'm sure he never let on to the press that he had a problem throwing away his lifelong dream to become Crown Prince of Monaco.

Does it bother him? He's so understanding and gentle toward me about finishing my degree.

I never held out any hopes of becoming a professional chemist, but he did plan to become a doctor. That must have hurt—a lot—but he's so nice about it. He turns his own loss into understanding and help for me.

I try to push those thoughts out of my head. None of that means anything. This marriage is just as fake as it was last night and at the wedding. It's a business transaction—nothing more.

I get up and go out to the apartment living room. The door to the other bedroom stands open. Christophe isn't here. I'm completely alone.

I wander around doing nothing in particular. I should call the kitchens and get them to send me my breakfast, but I can't decide what to ask for.

I go back to the bedroom, take a shower, and put on casual clothes for the day. I don't have anything else to do, so I unpack my suitcase and put everything in the dressers and closet. I guess I'll be staying here for a while.

I'm just finishing and wondering what to do next when the apartment door opens out in the living room. It opens without anyone knocking.

I expect it to be Christophe coming back, but it isn't. It's a tall man in his sixties and a middle-aged woman in her fifties.

They both wear business suits, stop in the middle of the floor, and the man bows to me. "Good morning, Your Highness," he tells me. "I trust you slept well."

"Uh….who are you?" I ask.

He bows again and shuts his eyes. "My name is Daniel Chevalier…."

"But everyone calls him Chevalier and you can, too," the woman interrupts. "He's your public affairs manager. He handles all your daily scheduled appointments, events, and state functions. He handles your whole schedule to make sure you accomplish everything and get to each event on time."

"Oh," I mumble. "I see."

"My name is Antoinette Dufrene, but you can call me Antoinette," the woman tells me. "I'm your stylist and wardrobe manager."

I open my mouth and start to say, "Uh….."

Antoinette cuts me off. "You have a state dinner to attend tonight at seven o'clock. It's an official celebration in honor of your wedding. You have appointments for your hair, nails, wardrobe, and makeup before that, but first you have another appointment with your wardrobe mistress to handle all your clothes."

"I already have enough clothes. I brought everything with me from home."

"Those are *your* clothes," Chevalier interrupts. "This appointment is for your official wardrobe—for all the clothes you'll wear to official state functions. Your wardrobe mistress handles all of that."

"And I'll be the one who decides what you wear to each event," Antoinette adds. "We have to make sure your style is on point for each one."

I'm still blinking at both of them when three waiters enter the room. One of them pushes what looks like a room service cart. Don't ask me what the other two waiters are doing here.

They park the cart next to the living room dining table and start laying out breakfast for me. "You better eat something before your wardrobe appointment," Chevalier tells me. "It's likely to be a long day."

"Um....where's Christophe?" I ask. "Won't I see him all day?"

"He's busy with matters of state with his father and brothers," Antoinette tells me. "You'll see him later at the dinner."

I guess I have to accept that. The three waiters all bow to me when I sit down at the table. I have to stop myself from bowing back at them. I don't know if I'll ever get used to this.

They slip out of the room and I start eating. Chevalier sits on the couch and starts making a million phone calls to people I don't know. He isn't talking about the official celebratory dinner tonight.

Antoinette pokes around the living room inspecting everything in detail. She doesn't look like she approves of anything.

She fingers the upholstery on the cushions, adjusts the position of chairs in the room, scowls at the patio and gardens outside, and even scrutinizes the curtains.

I try to keep my head down and eat my food without noticing the way the two of them are acting. They're here to manage me like some kind of show pony or something.

I should have expected this. I *did* expect it. I'm just in shock when I realize my life won't be my own anymore after this.

I almost dread asking Chevalier what appointments, obligations, and events I'll have to attend after tonight's dinner.

I find out all too soon when I finish eating and stand up from the table. The three waiters appear out of nowhere and start cleaning up.

Antoinette and Chevalier escort me out of the apartment. "Tomorrow morning, you and Christophe have an appearance at the charity hospital appeal conference to open the international debate.

At noon tomorrow, you'll both attend the opening match of the European badminton championships. At three o'clock, you're scheduled to attend a formal gathering of the Royal College of Engineers to commemorate the work of Gervais Gibeault……"

I don't hear anything else. Antoinette talks to me just as fast about every detail of my wardrobe. I don't understand half of what she says.

From what I can tell, she's talking about different color palettes, accent types, body shapes, and cuts of clothes that she thinks will flatter me the best.

I hate to admit that I never put that much thought into my clothes. The subject of what I would wear every day never seemed that complicated to me.

I guess it is now. What I wear is a matter of state. I follow them down the palace corridors—or rather they follow me down the palace corridors—but they don't really follow me.

They flank me on either side yammering into my ears the whole way. They distract me so much that I barely notice where we're going.

They turn off into a large room that's really one giant closet. Floor-to-ceiling closets cover every wall. Another side room branches off this one with more floor-to-ceiling closet space holding shoes, handbags, hats, and every kind of accessory known to the human race.

We meet up with a short, stout woman in her fifties. She's wearing the plainest, most ordinary outfit I've ever seen. Only the tips of her fluffy short hair have been dyed red. The rest of her hair closest to her head is pure white.

"This is Lucille Marchand, your wardrobe mistress," Antoinette tells me.

Lucille bows to me, but she smiles when she does it. Her eyes twinkle and she smiles cheerily. She's the first really cheery person I've met since I came here.

"So pleased to meet you, Your Highness!" she exclaims. "I can't wait to get started!"

"Um...thank you," I stammer. "Neither can I."

"We'll leave you alone," Chevalier tells me. "We'll come back in an hour to continue with your next appointment."

He and Antoinette leave me alone with Lucille. She starts fussing around the room as soon as the door closes.

"It's so wonderful to have you join us, Your Highness!" she gushes again. "We're going to have some fun today."

"I hope so," I remark. "At least I don't have to listen to any more schedule appointments."

She laughs. "Yes, there do seem to be a lot of them."

"I don't know when I'm ever going to have any free time. I didn't realize royal life would be this busy."

"Oh, it's busy, all right!" She comes toward me and starts tugging off the casual blazer I put on this morning. "Let's get this business started. Take this off....."

I slip out of the blazer. She grabs a measuring tape.

Like magic, half a dozen other people appear out of the woodwork and start buzzing around me the same way. Lucille measures up every part of me and calls the numbers over her shoulder.

The new people are all much younger than she is—except for one extremely old man who hobbles around with a walking stick. I can't even tell what all these other people are doing.

One youngish woman in her twenties scribbles on a clipboard and writes down all the measurements Lucille takes of me. She makes me stick out my arms, measures around my neck, and then down my legs.

The procedure takes a lot longer than I think it will. Lucille keeps walking around and around me adjusting this and that, straightening my clothes, and re-measuring the same things she measured before.

"All right. That's enough," she finally decides. "Come into the other room and we'll fit the dress you're going to wear tonight."

She leads the way to the right. I didn't notice before, but there's another section of the room over here.

A beautiful, magnificent, ornate ball gown hangs from a mannequin in the middle of the room. Lucille's helpers all swoop in and start pulling my clothes off in a whirlwind.

They do it so fast that I get dizzy. I'm too flustered to protest. I guess I'll have to get used to this, too.

They pull off my shirt, pants, shoes, socks, and even my bra. They fit me out with a strapless push-up bra that exaggerates my cleavage.

I should probably be self-conscious and embarrassed that a bunch of strangers are manhandling me like this, but the whole procedure feels so clinical that I can only stand here and tolerate it.

They take the dress off the mannequin and slip the gown over my head. It settles over my exposed chest and fits tightly around my waist when they button the clasps up my back.

Lucille moves in and starts adjusting and tugging at every part of the dress. She calls out instructions and more numbers to the young woman with the clipboard.

Lucille even sticks her fingers down my cleavage to reposition both the bra and the bodice of the dress. I would be embarrassed by that, but this whole process just makes me feel more like a piece of livestock going up for auction. I'm not really here.

I'm just another mannequin to display this dress. None of these people even see me.

Chapter 9: Geneviève

I take a few deep, steadying breaths before I walk into the grand dining room of the Royal Palace of Monaco. I've been here before, but only with my father and brothers.

I really wish Christophe was here. I would feel better walking into the event next to him instead of walking in by myself.

Antoinette, Chevalier, and all the other palace attendants keep telling me Christophe will meet me here, but I don't see him when I walk in.

I wouldn't be able to see him with so many people around. A bunch of strangers come over to greet me, bow to me, and congratulate me on my wedding.

The dress I tried on this morning fits better, but I still find myself dreading the moment when it slips down my chest and falls off. It won't, but I can't get rid of that irrational fear.

The dress looks as beautiful here as it did in Lucille's fitting room. Actually, the dress looks more beautiful. The lights shimmer on the lustrous fabric, but the dress doesn't look right without me standing next to someone.

I don't know what to do or who to talk to first, so I play it safe by going over to the Crown Prince and Princess Jasmine. I curtsey to them and tell them what an honor it is to attend this dinner.

Princess Jasmine smiles at me and pulls me over next to her. "You better stay here where you'll be safe from the vultures."

I gasp out a shaky, "Thank you!" and step into line with her and the Crown Prince. More people come over. They set up another receiving line of shaking my hand, bowing and curtseying to me, and some even kiss my hand.

"Where's Christophe?" I ask out the side of my mouth. "Everyone said he would meet me here."

"He's busy with palace business," Princess Jasmine tells me. "I'm sure he'll turn up later."

I glance toward the long table set with a million place settings. Where am I supposed to sit over there? Will I be sitting somewhere alone where it's obvious to all the guests that Christophe isn't here?

This position standing next to Princess Jasmine gives me a bird's-eye view of the rest of the dining room. The Crown Prince's sons Pascal and Renáld are here and so are all their cousins.

Pascal and Renáld stand in a huddle with Dorian, Casim, and Salvatore. The five of them talk and look around at the other guests. The cousins don't look in my direction.

Princesses Simone and Emeline come over to me with their cousins Johanne and Daphne. "Did Antoinette put the fear of God into you?" Simone asks.

"And let me guess," Emeline interjects. "Lucille practically put her fingers in your underwear when she tried to wedge you into that dress."

"Emeline!" Princess Jasmine chides. "Don't be so vulgar!"

The four cousins laugh. "You know it's true, Mother," Simone counters. "Lucille has no shame about sticking her fingers anywhere."

I find myself laughing nervously. "She wasn't the only one. Her minions practically gave me the full alien experimental examination."

The four cousins laugh like that's the funniest thing they ever heard.

"I'll bet your head is still spinning from Chevalier trying to tell you what your schedule will be," Emeline goes on.

"Try not to think about it," Simone tells me. "Just do what anyone tells you at any given moment. Don't think about anything beyond your next appointment."

I look around at all of them. "Really? That's a relief."

"He talks to himself out loud," Emeline goes on. "He recites the schedule to you so he can remember it. No one expects you to remember all of that."

"Wow," I murmur. "That makes it so much easier."

The two sisters swivel into line on my other side. Simone stands next to me with Emeline opposite her. Johanne gets involved in talking to someone else I don't know. Daphne disappears to the other side of the room.

"These events are really just an opportunity for all these people to show off their figures and impress everyone with their social skills," Simone tells me on the side. "None of this is about you. Just remember that. All you have to do is stand in the corner and look nice."

"Something tells me it's a little more complicated than that," I mumble.

"Of course it is. You have to talk to people, tell them what a pleasure it is to meet them, and sometimes listen to their ideas that they want to tell you about and maybe get you to invest in. All you have to do is look interested, tell them it's a really great idea, and you're certain they'll be able to accomplish it."

"What if they *can't* accomplish it? It isn't like I could invest in someone's idea on my own."

"That isn't the point. You're telling them you're certain *they* can accomplish it—as in by themselves with no help from you or the Royal Family. That's the whole reason they're telling you—to get you to invest in them. You're giving them a subtle hint that they have to do it themselves because you won't invest in them and neither will the Royal Family."

"Oh. I get it." I turn back to survey the room. "It is complicated."

"Not at all. Just go through the motions. Everything else will take care of itself."

Fortunately, we don't have to stand here looking beautiful for very much longer. The Crown Prince heads for the dining table. That's the signal for everyone else to sit down.

I find my place next to the Prince and Princess. The two places at the head of the table are labeled with mine and Christophe's names, but he still doesn't show up.

One of the butlers pulls out my chair for me to sit down. Crown Prince Gustav and Princess Jasmine sit side by side at the end of the table.

Christophe and I should be sitting in the first two places next to them, but the place between me and the Crown Prince stands empty. Christophe isn't here.

The butlers start serving the first course. Princess Jasmine talks to me about all the hair, nail, wardrobe, and makeup appointments I had to go through today to get ready for this dinner.

"Is it always like this?" I ask her.

She smiles kindly. She seems like a nice person. "It isn't usually as elaborate when you're going to tennis matches, polo tournaments, and think tank conferences. It always takes longer and more preparation when you have to dress formally and look glamorous."

I push my fork back and forth on my plate. "I don't know how you do it."

"You get used to it," she tells me. "You treat it like a job. You get up and go to your job every morning. That's the way I think of it." She turns to her husband. "Do you think of it that way?"

He nods. His deep eyes overflow with understanding when he looks at me. "Christophe told me about your desire to finish your degree, now that the wedding is behind you. I approve. You should continue your studies, but the security team will probably want you to do it remotely from the palace rather than attending the university every day. I'm sure Chevalier can accommodate any trips you need to make to meet with advisors and take examinations."

I can't look at him. "Thank you, Your Highness. You're too generous."

"Not at all. I wouldn't want you to break off your education because of something like this."

I don't know what to say, so I just mumble, "Thank you," again.

These people are all so nice. So why isn't Christophe here? None of them acts like his absence bothers them. None of them acts like they even notice his absence.

Wouldn't it be more important for him to make an appearance at this dinner than for me? He's the Crown Prince's heir. I'm only here because of Christophe.

No one mentions it. The butlers and servers don't serve him any food—as if he might show up any second now. They just ignore his place and serve me instead.

Sitting here alone feels more and more awkward as the evening-wears on. I can't be the only person who notices or cares that the guest of honor isn't here.

This dinner is supposed to be celebrating my wedding to Christophe. The dinner doesn't really work when only one of us is here.

I don't really have anyone else to talk to besides the Royal Couple. They make small talk. I do my best to make small talk back, but it feels forced. It is forced—on my part, at least.

They talk smoothly and easily like small talk is second nature to them. They make it look so easy.

The dinner drags on. Christophe still doesn't show up.

Then the Crown Prince and Princess Jasmine leave the table. Everyone mills around talking and socializing. The butlers carry drinks around to everyone. The evening wears on.

I lose track of who I'm talking to and who is even here. I talk to dozens of people I don't know. They all make small talk.

They talk about anything and everything except the fact that Christophe isn't here. I'm the only person who even notices or cares.

People finally start to drift away. I can finally excuse myself, take my leave from Prince Gustav and Princess Jasmine, and escape back to the apartment.

I don't know if I'm supposed to go back to Lucille's wardrobe room to take off this dress. No one tells me. I stick my head in there, but it's empty with all the lights turned off. I guess not.

I continue down the corridors to the apartment. At least I'll be able to take the dress off once I get inside.

I slip through the door, shut it behind me, and turn around.

I freeze dead in my tracks when someone else switches the light on. My blood runs cold when I find Christophe, his brothers, his cousins, and all their security men packed into the apartment living room.

Chapter 10: Christophe

I see the truth written all over Geneviève's face when she comes face to face with me, my brothers, cousins, and our security team assembled in the apartment living room.

She cringes away from us, but she has nowhere to run.

I take a step forward and drop the gun on the table. It's still covered in dirt from where she buried it out in the grounds.

The moisture from the soil hasn't pitted the metal after such a short time. The gun probably still works.

All the color drains from her face when she looks down at it. Of course she knows exactly where it came from.

"Do you mind explaining this to me?" I ask in a deadly undertone.

She opens her mouth and shuts it a few times before she can bring herself to make a sound. "I.....I didn't......"

"You had it with you at the wedding, didn't you?" Dorian snaps. "You must have hidden it under your dress."

"You planned to shoot Christophe, didn't you?" Casim interjects. "Just admit it so we can all get some sleep tonight."

"I didn't!" she practically shrieks. "I never wanted to bring the gun!"

"But you did bring it," Dorian counters. "It's a good thing he was wearing a bulletproof vest to his own wedding. He would be dead now....."

"NO!!" she screams. "I never wanted to do any of this! I was getting out of the limo to go into the cathedral and Raoul pushed the gun into my hand. He told me......"

"What?" I ask. "He told you what? He told you to shoot me?"

Her eyes dart away and her features spasm.

"Just tell the truth," Dorian snarls. "Don't waste our time by lying about it."

"Yes!" she blurts out. "He told me to shoot Christophe—but I couldn't! I swear it! What was I supposed to do? I had to hide the gun somewhere! I couldn't let my sisters see it—and I couldn't hide it in the rectory, could I? I had to scramble to put it somewhere before someone saw it—so I put it in my garter—but I never planned to use it! I swear!"

"How can we believe that?" Casim demands. "Your family concocted this whole wedding to get you inside the palace so you could kill the Crown Prince's heir. Admit it."

"No! I mean....." She flaps her hands in nervous agitation. "I don't know, okay? I don't know if my father came up with this arranged marriage for that reason! I didn't know anything about this until Remi and Raoul gave me the gun. Then what was I supposed to do? I wasn't alone until after we came back here. I hid it in the only place I could think." She squirms right and left, looks everywhere but at me, and wrings her hands. "Now Raoul and Remi will kill me because I betrayed the family!"

Those words twist the knife in my guts. Knowing she brought a gun into the palace to shoot me doesn't mean as much as knowing the reason why.

Dorian takes a step forward. "You're under arrest—just in case you weren't quite sure. You're damn lucky we don't execute you right now...."

My arm shoots out to stop him. "Hold it."

She flies into hysterics when she hears him. "You have to believe me! Please, Christophe! I swear I never wanted to kill you! That's why I hid the gun. I didn't know what else to do! My father would have a fit if I told you—and I never even got a chance to tell you! The first time I could have told you was in the limo—and then....."

She breaks off and I realize what she means. She must have been freaking out when she saw me wearing a bulletproof vest.

She must have been freaking out even before that. I can just picture the sequence of events.

She must have been losing her mind when she had to carry the gun into the cathedral and then go through the whole ceremony with it hidden under her dress.

She's right—if she's telling the truth. She never had a chance to tell me—and her father and brothers would have been livid if she did tell me.

What exactly was she supposed to do with it? It wasn't like I gave her a whole lot of confidence to open up to me after we came home from the church. When would she have told me? *How* would she have told me?

Dorian spins around and glares at me. "You can't seriously believe this line of bullshit, do you? She's faking! She's an actress!"

"NO!!" She starts shaking like a leaf. "I'm not making it up! Remi said they would station someone outside the garden wall—on the other side of the bench at the end of the avenue. He said I could get out of the apartment through the patio doors after I shot you, run down the avenue, and climb over the wall. He said his and Raoul's people would get me out of the city and into hiding before anyone caught me. You should be able to find the person on your security camera feeds. I'm not making it up! I swear it! You have to believe me."

"You would say anything to save your own neck," Casim snaps.

I can't stand that. I spin around and wave at all the men in the room. "Everybody out. Clear the room. I want to talk to Geneviève alone."

"That's a terrible idea," Salvatore tells me.

"Just let me handle this, all right?" I wave to all the security guys. "You can station people outside the room. Then you can break in if you hear any sounds of a scuffle."

"What about gunshots?" Renáld asks.

I hand him the gun. "Take this with you. Everything will be all right. Just leave me alone with her."

They take a long time to leave. Pascal gives me a searching look before he follows Renáld and my cousins out of the room.

What would Pascal do in this situation? I know he backs me every step of the way.

He wouldn't arrest Geneviève and he definitely wouldn't execute her. He would find out what's going on beneath the surface.

That's what I have to do. Dorian is a hothead and Casim is a hardass. I value all my cousins, but I have to take the middle approach.

Geneviève stands there trembling in her shoes while the guys file out of the room one at a time. Dorian and Casim glare at her. Renáld doesn't look at her at all.

Pascal gives her the same searching look. I almost wish I could keep him in the room with me when I question her. I need his steadying influence right now.

I can't do that. I need to question Geneviève alone.

She won't look at me while they leave. She won't look at me even after the door shuts.

I take a few steps forward and stop in front of her. She keeps fidgeting, squirming, and twisting her knuckles together in nervous anxiety.

"Don't worry," I murmur. "No one is going to hurt you."

"You have to believe me!" Her voice trembles and she looks down at her white knuckles. "I swear I never planned any of this! He forced me to take the gun just a few seconds before I walked into the church. I'm telling you the truth!"

"I believe you." I would be stupid not to considering how terrified she is.

That's the moment I remember how terrified she looked through the whole wedding service. She was going out of her mind through the whole reception, through the whole limo ride back to the palace, and the whole time she and I were alone in this apartment.

Her behavior makes so much more sense now. I can't help but believe her when I remember all of that. Her story is the only logical explanation for the way she acted that day.

"I just need to know if you ever planned to use the gun after that day," I go on. "Did you plan to dig up the gun later?"

"No!" Her voice breaks, but she doesn't start crying. She's too agitated even for that. "I just wanted to get rid of it—somewhere you would never find it! I didn't want.....I didn't want......"

She doesn't finish. She didn't want to face the exact same accusations she's facing right now.

"I thought the gun would rot and rust in the ground," she chokes. "That's why I didn't try to protect it when I buried it. I just wanted it to disappear...I couldn't think of anywhere else to put it.....and now....."

She looks away toward the other side of the room.

Facing our accusations won't be nearly as bad as facing her father and brothers. They will definitely not be pleased that she failed to go through with the plan.

"I believe you." I take a chance and slip my hand into hers. "Nothing is going to happen to you. No one is going to hurt you. I promise."

She doesn't even notice that I'm touching her. "I'm sorry!" she quavers. "I know I should have told you! I just didn't know how to do that without making the situation worse between you and my brothers—and then you and I......things were so hostile between us....I couldn't tell you......and then once I buried the gun......it seemed better to just pretend it wasn't there......"

"Okay, that's enough. You don't have to try to convince me. I believe you. It's over."

She won't stop looking around. "I don't understand. What are you going to do?"

"That's for me to decide. I want you to go to your room, change your clothes, and go to bed."

Her head shoots up. "What?"

"Go to bed—alone this time. Go to your room, change out of your dress, put on your pajamas, get into bed, turn off the light, and go to sleep. I'll deal with this."

"But.....what about....what about Raoul?"

"Don't worry about Raoul. He doesn't concern you right now. Go on, Geneviève. Go to bed."

She still hesitates. She barely even hears me.

I give it up and tow her to the bedroom door by her hand. I stop there and give her a gentle push toward the open doorway. "Go," I tell her. "Go to bed."

She blinks around in confusion and finally steps into the room. I shut the door behind her and leave her there alone before I walk out of the apartment.

I find my brothers, cousins, and our security guys all crowded in the corridor outside. None of them left.

"What did she say?" Pascal asks.

"She says she wanted the gun to rot in the ground and disappear. That's why she didn't wrap it up or try to protect it from the soil."

"And you actually believe that?" Dorian snaps.

"Yes, I believe it. You all saw the way she was acting at the wedding and the reception. She was terrified out of her wits. What other explanation is there than that she was worried about someone catching her with the gun?"

"Maybe she was just nervous about the wedding," Renáld replies.

"She wasn't nervous about the wedding," Pascal counters. "She wasn't nervous at the original negotiation dinner and she wasn't nervous when she and Christophe met in the drawing room. She wasn't happy about the wedding, but she wasn't nervous and she wasn't scared—not like she was the wedding itself."

"She was more scared at the reception than she was at the wedding," I go on. "Even if she was nervous about the wedding, her nerves should have started to go down after it was all over. They didn't. They got worse—and then they were at their worst in the limo on the way back here and they got to a breaking point once we came here and we were alone together. The gun is the only explanation."

"What are you going to do?" Salvatore asks. "You can't trust her not to try something else."

"I'm going to give her a chance to prove herself. If I'm right about her, she won't try something else. She never wanted to try anything in the first place—not anything as drastic as that."

"You're playing games with your life," Casim tells me. "You should get rid of her."

"No one is getting rid of her—and I don't want to hear any of you threatening her again—not with anything—not even arrest. You can arrest her only if you can prove to me that she actually committed a crime."

"Bringing a gun into the palace is a crime," Salvatore interjects. "What are you going to do about that?"

"I just told you what I'm going to do. She told the truth about being in danger from her brothers if she didn't carry out the plan."

"At least post a guard outside the apartment in case something happens," Dorian tells me.

"No, no guards. All of you go back to what you were doing. I'll deal with her."

Dorian and Casim shake their heads before they walk away cursing under their breath. Salvatore and the security guys leave a few minutes later. Renáld goes with them.

Pascal waits until last and squeezes my shoulder. "You did the right thing," he tells me.

I mumble, "Thanks," and he walks off. I knew he would approve.

Something happened to him. Everyone ignores him and pretends he isn't there. The press never focuses on him. They barely even mention him.

Standing in the background of everything makes him especially observant. No one outside the family ever tries to talk to him.

He sees and understands more about people than I'll ever learn in a lifetime. He sees the true nature of people.

It isn't even so much that he always sees the good in people because he doesn't always.

He sees what's true about a person. If he thinks someone is good or innocent, he's pretty much always right.

If he thinks someone is a lying manipulative bastard, he's pretty much always right about that, too.

I would like to question him more about what he sees in Geneviève, but he basically just told me. He thinks she's innocent, too. He believes her when she says she didn't plan this.

I wait until everyone leaves before I go back into the apartment. I press my ear to Geneviève's bedroom door. I don't hear anything, so I ease the door open.

She lies asleep in bed with the covers over her. Good. She needs rest. I don't know what tomorrow will bring, but she needs to pull her head together after this.

I sit in the living room for a while and bring up the security camera feeds on my phone.

I scroll back to the time stamps of Geneviève and me coming home from the reception. I mark the time stamp and check the feeds from outside the palace walls.

I roll to the footage beyond the bench at the end of the avenue. I checked that when I saw her burying the gun.

I didn't see anything then, but I didn't know what to look for. I locate the same people on the opposite sidewalk. They take pictures of the palace and the surrounding architecture.

I didn't see anything suspicious in anyone's behavior then and I don't see anything suspicious in their behavior now—not until I keep rolling the footage forward.

The same four guys pace up and down the block, turn the corner, come back, and stand out there taking more pictures of exactly the same scenery.

They stay for more than two hours after she buries the gun. Those four guys never leave—not entirely. They must be the people waiting to take her into hiding.

I double-check by rolling back the footage to before she buried the gun. The same four guys stood outside the palace through the whole reception. They were there long before Geneviève and I came back.

Those guys could only be waiting for her. She's right. This proves she's telling the truth.

I put my phone away and lean back on the couch to think about it. Now I have to figure out what to do about this.

It isn't such a nice feeling to know an entire group of people is out there plotting to kill me right now.

Chapter 11: Geneviève

I snap awake in the dark. I sit bolt upright in bed and look all around me before I remember where I am. I'm in the apartment in the Royal Palace. I'm alone again.

I'm wearing my pajamas. I'm comfortable in bed, but I can't settle down.

Christophe isn't here, but something's wrong. I can't put my finger on it.

My eyes adjust to the darkness. I don't see anything out of the ordinary—not that I'm used to seeing this place in darkness.

The door to my bedroom is still shut. Is Christophe out there?

I slip out of bed, open the door, and pad into the living room in my bare feet. It's empty, too.

The door of his room stands open. The bed is still made. He isn't anywhere in the apartment. He didn't sleep here.

I stop in the middle of the living room to look around at everything. I still get the feeling something is wrong. Is someone watching me?

That's just paranoia. This palace has more security than the Vatican. Maybe I had a bad dream or something.

I slip back into my bedroom to go back to sleep. I walk around the bed to my side. I jump back and stifle a scream when Raoul steps out from behind the curtains. He's inside my bedroom!

"What are you doing here?!" I hiss. "You scared the life out of me!"

"You didn't do what I told you to do," he growls. "I gave you that gun to shoot Christophe, but you didn't do it."

"You're right!" I blurt out. "He and his cousins were already onto your plan! He was wearing a bulletproof vest under his tux at the wedding—and I couldn't do it after we got back here."

"Why not? Was he still wearing the vest? Don't tell me he's been wearing a bulletproof vest around you here in his own palace."

"They would have killed me if I didn't back out on the plan when I did...."

"You're lying!" he snaps. "You're a traitorous slut who betrayed your own family!"

"You put me in an impossible situation—and his cousins would execute me if they knew I brought a gun into the palace! You're the one who betrayed me—not the other way around!"

"You sold out your own family to our enemies......"

"Papa arranged this marriage to make peace with the Royal Family! Don't you understand that? Are you really telling me he was behind this plot from the beginning so he could kill Christophe? Why don't you get me executed for real by getting me to shoot the Crown Prince himself?!"

"Striking a blow for the family is more important than your life!" he snaps back. "You should have gone through with the plan even if it meant dying."

My jaw drops. "You can't be serious!"

"If you don't do it, maybe we should consider *you* an enemy of our family."

My throat goes dry. I have difficulty swallowing down my shocked horror. "Are you saying what I think you're saying?"

"Find a way to carry out the plan. You still have the gun. Find a way to kill Christophe or I'll do it myself. If you don't, I'll know which side you're really on and I'll have to come back and take care of both of you."

I can only stand there with my mouth hanging open when he slips out the patio door and vanishes into the grounds.

I knew Raoul and Remi were dangerous. I never dreamed they could be this dangerous.

Raoul threatened me. He still expects me to kill Christophe one way or the other.

He doesn't know I don't have the gun anymore. I suppose I could find some other way to kill Christophe.

This apartment has a small kitchenette in the living room. I could use one of the kitchen knives to stab him or cut his throat. That part would be easy—except that I don't plan to kill anyone.

Raoul threatened me. That tells me all I need to know about him, Remi, and anyone else who agrees with them.

Those words say it all. *Striking a blow for the family is more important than your life. You should have gone through with the plan even if it meant dying.*

My own brothers don't care about me. They would gladly sacrifice me.....and for what? What would killing Christophe actually accomplish?

What does striking a blow for our family even mean? This so-called feud between the Lefebvres and the Royal Family—it doesn't mean anything.

The feud hasn't been any kind of violent conflict—not for centuries—if it ever was a violent conflict. No one left alive can even remember how the feud started.

The two families just hate each other from a distance. That's as far as it ever goes—until now.

Is that what Raoul wants me to throw my life away for?

This man isn't my brother. These people aren't my family. We don't have a family if they could throw away my life so easily—for nothing.

I stand there staring out the window. All these thoughts collide in my head. Now what am I supposed to do with all of this?

Chapter 12: Christophe

I point at a map of the palace grounds on the computer in the palace security office.

"We already have enough guys stationed outside the walls. We can't post any more of them without turning the palace into a fortified garrison—and I don't want security personnel stopping and questioning every tourist on the street. Monaco is supposed to be a relaxing haven where people can get away from it all—not a Police state."

"Then the only other place to put our guys is inside the grounds and inside the corridors themselves," Casim tells me.

I shake my head. "Then we would turn the palace into a fortified garrison, too. There must be another way."

"At least take armed security with you," Salvatore suggests.

"When I'm walking around my own house? Is that really necessary?" I bend over the map. "We already take armed security when we go out in public. Having them follow us around inside would be overkill."

"Or just kill," Dorian adds. "Isn't that what we're talking about—someone trying to kill you?"

My brother Pascal calls from the other side of the room. He stands at one of the banks of security camera displays behind me.

"Christophe!" he calls. "You better take a look at this." I go over to him. He points at a feed from the gardens. "Raoul Lefebvre is inside the grounds. The camera just picked him up coming from the patio of your apartment."

Casim, Salvatore, and Dorian all spin away from the table where we've just been going over the security arrangements for the palace.

"Let's go!" Dorian barks to the surrounding guards. "Get out there and track him down. Consider him armed and dangerous!"

The security guys stop off at the weapons locker on their way out of the room. Each man grabs a rifle or a shotgun, checks the magazine, and moves on to make room for more men coming in behind them.

Some of the men grab night-vision or motion-sensing glasses so we'll be able to see Raoul in the dark grounds.

Each of these guys already carries more than one concealed sidearm. We won't be short on firepower when we find Raoul.

My brothers and cousins all arm themselves, too. I grab a shotgun and stick a carton of shells in my jacket pocket before I follow the others outside.

We don't turn on any lights as we pass down the palace corridors. We don't want to tip off Raoul that we're coming after him.

I can't wait to question that prick about what he told Geneviève. I don't really need confirmation that he gave her the gun and told her to kill me. I just want to see the bastard's face when he admits it.

He must have made contact with her just now in the apartment—either for good or bad. We're going to get some answers tonight one way or the other.

Our group slips into the grounds through the terrace foyer. Everything sounds quiet. I can't see much in the dark.

Dorian waves to all of us to spread out. I head over to the patio outside my apartment and look through into the living room and the bedroom.

Moonlight floods the living room. It's empty and quiet. The curtains are closed in the bedroom. I can't see anything in there. The curtains were closed when I looked in on Geneviève earlier, so that's nothing unusual.

I follow the trail where Pascal showed me Raoul leaving the apartment. He went back toward the bench at the end of the avenue.

I don't see or hear anything there. The security guys sweep the whole area. They pass their night-vision and motion-sensing glasses over everything.

Most of these guys have night-vision scopes on their weapons, too. The team should find Raoul if he's still out here.

I meet up with the other guys near the terrace fountain. "We aren't picking up any sign of him," Salvatore tells me. "He could have slipped out while we were on the way over here."

"He may have just come to make contact with Geneviève," I tell him. "Pull the team back to the office. Tell them to sweep the palace just to make sure he really is gone."

We all go back to the security office and hang up our weapons. I say good night to everyone and head for my apartment. It's already four o'clock in the morning, but I'm not tired. I need to question Geneviève about Raoul's visit. He couldn't have come for any good reason.

I climb down the stairs and pass through a bunch of different corridors before I enter the residential wing. My parents, brothers, sisters, cousins, and aunt each live in their own suite apartment.

Did Raoul give Geneviève another weapon? Is that what I can look forward to when I get back to my apartment—gunshots to the face?

Maybe my cousins are right and I'm being way too casual about this. Maybe we really do need security right here inside the palace.

I hate to think of turning the palace into that, but the building isn't safe if Raoul can break in so easily.

My mind goes back to the map of the grounds and surrounding area. My brothers, cousins, and I have always taken charge of security, but maybe it's time to bring in the experts.

I don't even know where I would begin to look for someone like that. I would have to check with some other heads of state. Maybe they can recommend someone.

Whoever it is needs to have experience guarding heads of state. I don't want to hire any old mercenaries off the street. That would be terrible.

I barely notice where I am or what I'm doing when something collides with me from the side. I barely turn a corner and snap out of my trance in time before a person tackles me across the floor, pins me down, and grabs me by the throat.

I stare up in shock at Raoul Lefebvre straddling my chest. He crushes my throat in one hand and swings a handgun around with the other to aim at my head.

I'm so stunned that I don't react for a second—not until he actually does point the gun at my head.

I knock the gun out of the way just as it goes off, but he corrects and brings it back just as fast.

I wake up to the reality of my situation in time to take my other hand off his wrist and grab his gun in both of my hands. I wrench it out of the way, but he's a lot bigger and stronger than I am.

We get into a wrestling match over the gun, but I can't use as much of my weight when he's sitting on top of me like this.

I yank and grapple for control of the weapon. It goes off again and fires straight into the floor a few inches away from my head. I have to do something before he kills me for real.

I throw one of my legs up and knee him in the back, but that only infuriates him. He roars at me through bared teeth and doubles down on his strength to twist the weapon back toward me.

The situation disintegrates before my eyes. The gunshots should bring my brothers and cousins running, but not fast enough. Maybe they were too far away to hear.

I feel my arms starting to weaken when another flying missile rockets out of nowhere, smashes into Raoul, and bowls him off me.

I stare in abject shock as Geneviève tumbles over and over her brother. She's still wearing her pajamas. She must have just come from the apartment.

They somersault away and crash into the wall right next to a pedestal with a large vase of flowers on it.

Their bodies bump the pedestal and it topples right next to them. The vase bounces off Raoul's shoulder and falls swiveling in circles on the floor.

All the flowers scatter and water starts gurgling from the mouth of the vase, but Geneviève doesn't notice any of that.

She seizes the vase, raises it, and smashes it down with all her strength into her brother's face. She crushes his nose and then hits him again and again screaming in a wild, hysterical frenzy.

I only realize a second too late that she's hitting him way too hard. I scramble onto my knees and hustle over there to grab her arms. "Enough!" I yell. "That's enough! He's out cold! Stop! You don't have to hit him anymore!"

I have to time my movements to restrain her arms. She struggles for a second and then realizes what she's doing.

She looks up at me in insane panic, drops the vase, and then tears out of my arms to pounce on her brother.

She grabs his shirt and tries to shake him. "No! No! You have to wake up!"

I look down at Raoul just as my brothers and cousins come running around the corner fully armed. They slow down when they see Raoul lying there with his face smashed in.

He lies way too still. He isn't breathing anymore. His skull doesn't look intact enough for anyone to survive this.

Geneviève keeps trying to pick him up. His weight pulls him down and his broken skull lolls on the tile floor. A puddle of blood surrounds his head underneath. Man, she must have really hit him hard.

I struggle to my feet and pull her away. "Come on. Come back to the apartment."

She spins around and starts shrieking in my face. "He threatened me, Christophe!" she screams. "He broke into the apartment and threatened me! He said he would kill me if I didn't finish the job! You have to believe me!"

"Okay," I murmur. "I believe you. Now come on."

She won't stop blabbering about how Raoul broke into the apartment and threatened her. I pull her farther down the corridor toward the apartment.

My brothers and cousins advance more slowly toward Raoul's body. None of them does first aid on him.

Pascal squats down and checks Raoul's pulse. They don't swoop in to start CPR. It must all be over. She killed him.

I really hope Geneviève doesn't see everything my brothers aren't doing, but I can't really stop her from seeing.

I try to turn her away, but she's so out of her mind that she doesn't cooperate. I finally push open the apartment door and steer her into the living room.

I sit her on the couch, but she won't sit still. "You have to believe me, Christophe!" she tells me again. "He was right here in the apartment—in my bedroom!"

"I do believe you, sweetheart," I murmur. "We saw him leave the apartment on the camera feed."

She still doesn't hear me. She passes her hand across her brow and grimaces in turmoil. "Remi is going to kill me for this! Oh, my God! What will Papa say when he finds out?!"

"He doesn't have to find out. We'll put out a press release that the security team caught Raoul on the grounds and they put him down before they realized who it really was."

She looks up and makes full eye contact with me for the first time. Her features spasm all over the place and she can't control her mouth. "He's dead, isn't he?! He's dead! I killed Raoul! Oh, my God! I killed Raoul!"

"Hey! Easy!" I pull her into my arms and hold her, but she's shaking too badly. "Everything is going to be all right. You did the right thing. No one can blame you for what you did."

She huddles against my chest trembling all over. Her voice breaks an octave higher. "He said he was going to kill me! He said I was an enemy of the family if I didn't finish the job."

I can't stop myself from bending down and kissing her hair. She saved my life. I know that now.

It cost her something she might never be able to afford. She might never get over this.

I have to take care of her and make sure everything works out for her. I can't let her suffer because of this.

I push her back to sit her up. "Come here. You need to go back to bed."

She doesn't move. She barely responds to anything I say. This whole thing must be breaking her last nerve.

Her knees turn to water when I try to stand her up. I wind up wrapping my arms around her and then picking her up completely.

I carry her into the bedroom. Her side of the bed is still messed up with the covers thrown back.

Raoul didn't enter the grounds until after midnight. He must have woken her up—the cocksucker.

It doesn't matter because he's dead. Now we have to deal with Remi and maybe their father.

She whimpers when I lower her onto the sheets. I try to put her down, but she won't stop clinging to me. She lets out these little pathetic mews of anguish every time she breathes.

She sounds so heartbroken and terrified, but she still doesn't cry. I can't bring myself to pull her arms off me, so I slip into bed next to her.

I'm still fully dressed. I don't plan to do anything with her like this—not that I was thinking about doing anything with her anyway.

I pull the covers up and tuck them around her. She sinks all the way against me, now that she's comfortable.

I hold her with one arm while I pull my phone out with the other. She falls back to sleep while I text Pascal about what's going on out there.

The medical team just checked Raoul. He's gone.

I text him back. *Pass it around to the press that the security team killed him. I don't want this getting back to her.*

Of course. I understand.

He doesn't have to say anything else. Of course he understands. He was the only other person besides me who stood up for her.

The others will come around about her now. She killed her own brother to save my life. That counts for a lot in this family.

I send a few more texts to my cousins and the rest of the team. *Scrub all the security camera footage of the fight. We'll keep it in the vault where it can't fall into the wrong hands.*

Where should we tell the press he died? Dorian asks. *If we say he died in the grounds, the press will want to see footage of that.*

We'll tell them it happened in the trees and the darkness and the undergrowth blocked the cameras.

We need to alert the Police, Pascal tells me. *They'll need to investigate.*

Just brief the security team beforehand so they all give the same story.

Who should we say killed Raoul? Casim asks.

Ask the guys for volunteers, I tell him. *Offer a fat bonus to anyone who takes the credit.*

Renáld breaks in on the conversation. *I'll do it. I'll tell them he was attacking you in the trees and I hit him in the face with a fallen log. That should satisfy them.*

Thank you, brother, I tell him. *Take the security team out to the trees and decide where it happened, where you got the log, and trample the area with plenty of footprints to make it look believable. Then you can call the Police.*

We'll take care of it, Pascal adds. *You take care of Geneviève.*

I smile at the screen. *I will.*

I put my phone away and settle down in bed. She's already sound asleep.

I don't want anyone finding out about this. She's going to have a hard enough time getting over this without the press making it a thousand times worse.

Chapter 13: Geneviève

I wake up to sunshine streaming through the bedroom windows. The curtains are open, but something isn't right.

I realize what it is when I feel a man's body lying next to me. I jolt when I realize it's Christophe. He's sound asleep. His chest rises and falls right under my cheek. I must have been sleeping on top of him.

His arm rests around my shoulders. He sleeps with his head turned in the other direction. He's still fully dressed and his body feels soft and completely relaxed.

I don't feel right about lying this close to him. I remember him comforting me last night and even getting into bed with me, but that was different. I was too upset about Raoul.

I pull out of Christophe's arms and sit up on the edge of the bed. How am I supposed to deal with Christophe after we just spent the night together?

I can't deny that we really did spend the night together this time. He didn't bail after I went to sleep. Now I'm sitting up and I have no choice but to face the reality of what I did last night. I killed Raoul.

He attacked Christophe and tried to shoot him. I'm sure the palace maintenance team is out there replacing the floor tiles Raoul destroyed with gunshots. That could have been Christophe's head.

How am I supposed to deal with this? What if Remi and my father find out that I'm the one who killed Raoul?

Getting out of bed wakes up Christophe. He sighs, shifts his weight under the covers, and then groans.

He gasps a few times and runs his fingers through his hair before he looks around and remembers where he is and why.

I can't look at him. I don't know who I am or what I'm doing with my life. What kind of person am I that could kill my own brother? How did any of this happen?

Christophe rolls in my direction and rests his hand on my back. I have to stop myself from recoiling from his touch.

"Are you okay?" he murmurs.

I shrug and look down at my hands. "I don't even know what that means anymore. I don't know what my life would look like if I was okay."

"No one will find out about this," he tells me. "We're going to scrub the security camera footage and tell the press that the security team put down Raoul. Renáld is going to tell the Police that he hit Raoul with a log when Raoul attacked me. No one will ever find out that you were involved."

I wind up squirming again. I can only mumble, "Thanks."

He props himself up on his elbow and talks right behind me. "The security around you is going to get a lot stricter from now on. I just want you to understand the situation we're in now. Your father, Remi, Marcel—we don't know if any of them are involved in this or which of them are involved in this. Any of them could come after you again."

I nod at nothing. "I understand."

"We'll cancel most of your appointments and appearances. The ones we can't cancel will have to be reworked to accommodate additional security. Your family will probably escalate these attacks even while they're pretending to make allies of my family on the surface."

Now it's my turn to groan. I cover my eyes. "I can't believe this is happening! I can't believe I'm actually caught in the middle of all of this!"

He reclines back on the pillows. "You'll have to spend a lot more time inside the palace and even inside this apartment. I know it will be hard for you not to get out as much, but your safety is more important until we can find another solution."

"What other solution would that be?"

He shrugs. "I can't think of one right now, but maybe something will come up."

I turn around to look at him. I wind up looking down at him from directly above. "You don't think.....?"

I stop myself from saying it. I don't even know what I was going to ask.

I don't know where I stand with him, either. He's a stranger, but last night brought us closer together.

This is the second time we've spent the night together in the same bed—without taking our clothes off. Should I read anything into that?

He stares up at me from below. He's still lying flat on his back completely relaxed on the pillow.

I find myself looking deep into his eyes trying to figure out......I don't know what I'm trying to figure out.

I still don't understand my thoughts or feelings when he raises his hand, cups the side of my head, and pulls me down to kiss me.

I get lost in that kiss. I don't know why, but it doesn't surprise me. Maybe it's all these times I've fallen asleep with him these last few days—or maybe it's the fact that we're already married.

His other hand closes around the other side of my face. His fingers slip into my hair. He doesn't stop kissing me. He escalates until our mouths open and our tongues meet in a sea of blissful warmth.

None of this shocks or surprises me—almost as if it came naturally to both of us or we were both already thinking it.

I wasn't and I know he wasn't, either. It just happened, but now it feels good and right and comfortable. Kissing him feels normal—like I never should have been doing anything else.

I don't know the moment when it happens, but something switches in me. My body or maybe some force outside of me tears me away from him.

I don't think. Thinking isn't part of this.

I actually enjoyed kissing him. I didn't want to stop, but whatever this is won't let me.

I stand up, turn away, and walk across the room. "I should take a shower. I don't want anyone to walk in on me looking like this. I can just imagine what your brothers and cousins thought when they saw me in my pajamas last night."

"No one thought anything—except that you were extremely brave for coming out of nowhere the way you did."

I can't look at him. I can't talk about or even think about last night.

I grab my clothes out of the dresser, snatch a few things from the closet, and barricade myself in the bathroom. I didn't just kiss Christophe, but that's nothing compared to what I did last night.

None of that happened. I'm not thinking about that. I turn on the shower, slip out of my pajamas, and get in. I need to do anything to take my mind off of....well, everything.

I get out of the shower and leave the bathroom while I dry my hair. Christophe isn't in the bedroom anymore.

I open the bedroom door and hear the shower running in his bathroom on the other side of the living room. I find myself smiling when I realize he's right there on the other side of the apartment.

I don't know why his presence makes me feel better, but it does.

I finish my hair. I'm sitting in the living room painting my toenails when he comes out wearing a pair of pants from what looks like a suit. He isn't wearing a shirt or shoes and his wet hair is a mess.

I stop myself from looking at his bare chest and shoulders. He's stunning and looks even better with his dark hair hanging over his eyes.

"I ordered breakfast," he tells me. "They should be bringing it any....."

He breaks off when the servers wheel in the cart with our food on it.

He answers the door without his shirt on. The servers set the table for us while he finishes getting dressed and combs his hair.

He sits down across from me. "I want you to stay in the apartment today," he tells me. "At least until we're certain we have the situation contained."

I don't even have to ask what he means. I stare down at my plate. I don't feel very hungry all of a sudden. "Whatever you think is best," I mumble. "I'm sorry I'm causing your family so many problems."

"Make that the last time you ever apologize for anything that happened last night," he snaps. "You saved my life. Everyone in the family is beyond grateful to you for what you did—and I'm beyond grateful. Don't apologize. All of this is peanuts compared to what you did for us—for me. None of us will ever forget that."

I can't look up. I really wish I could.

I hate myself for killing Raoul. I shouldn't. I know he was the one who did this and I was protecting Christophe. I still can't help blaming myself.

I don't want to look up and see in Christophe's eyes that he understands how I feel. I'm certain he does—especially after the way he took care of me last night.

I don't want anyone feeling sorry for me. I don't want anyone taking any special precautions for me. I don't want to be part of this at all.

He keeps eating while he waits a long time for me to say something. "I'll get Chevalier to send you a computer with an internet connection," he goes on. "You can start researching what it will take to transfer your credits here so you can restart your schooling."

I can only mumble, "Thanks." I'm too grateful for his care and kindness.

I really wish I could talk to him about all of this, but that would mean I would actually have to deal with everything that happened. I'm not ready for that.

He finishes first, puts on his jacket, and comes over to me while I'm still sitting at the table. He kisses me on the side of the head.

"Try not to get too bored today. I'll come back this evening and we'll talk before dinner together—just the two of us. You don't have to go out and deal with the rest of the world."

Chapter 14: Geneviève

C hristophe walks out of the apartment and shuts the door behind him. Now I'm all alone, but it feels better like this. I don't want to see anyone else right now. I don't want to talk to anyone, especially not anyone who knows about last night.

I must still be exhausted, not just from all the stress of the wedding and the whole gun incident, but also from staying up too much last night. I didn't get enough sleep.

I finish breakfast, load all the dirty dishes back onto the cart, and push it out into the corridor. I've seen a few others sitting outside different bedrooms. This seems to be how the Royal Family deals with their dishes if they eat in their rooms or apartments.

I go back inside, tidy up, put my clothes and pajamas away, and hang up my dress from last night's official dinner.

I never want to see that dress again. It reminds me of my confrontation with Christophe and his brothers and cousins over the gun. That dress will always remind me of Dorian threatening to arrest me and maybe even execute me.

I dread the day I have to see any of them again. They all know about me. They all know I killed Raoul.

Christophe's words that his family is grateful—those words don't penetrate my shattered brain. Maybe I'm too tired to believe him.

I bring my phone into the living room and recline on the couch to catch up on my emails and social media comments, but my fatigue catches up with me and I wind up falling asleep.

I'm still lying there when someone knocks on the door. It can't be Christophe. Antoinette and Chevalier don't knock, either.

I frown to myself while I blink the sleep out of my eyes. I rub my face and drag myself over there to see who it is.

I open the door and scowl while I try to understand what I'm seeing. Christophe's sisters Simone and Emeline stand there grinning at me. Simone holds a laptop under her arm.

"Hi," she greets me.

"Um....hi." I look back and forth between them. "Can I help you?"

"I doubt it." Simone takes a step forward, shoves the computer into my hands, and brushes past me to enter the apartment. Emeline does the same thing without giving me a computer.

Simone throws herself down into one of the armchairs in the living room. "Christophe asked us to stop by and keep you company—since you're under lockdown in here. He thought you might need someone to talk to—and he asked me to bring you that computer so you can start looking into continuing your studies."

Emeline squints through the patio windows. "Isn't it boring being stuck inside all the time? The guys won't let us out of the house, either."

I shut the door, put the laptop on the table, and go over to sit on the couch. "At least you aren't confined to your rooms."

"That's what we're here for," Simone tells me.

"Just don't practice your MMA skills on us," Emeline adds. "We're fragile."

"Emeline!" Simone exclaims. "Leave her alone! Don't make fun of her."

I look away. "So everyone knows, don't they?"

"Not everyone," Simone replies. "Just a few key people. It won't go beyond the family—and one or two trusted security guys who helped scrub the video record files."

"You guys are really nice," I murmur. "I'm grateful to you for coming over."

I keep it to myself that I'm over-the-top grateful to Christophe for everything he's doing for me.

"We're the ones who are grateful to you." Emeline sits down next to me and bends forward to peer into my face. "I really admire what you did last night. That's all I was trying to say. I'm sorry if it came out wrong. I could never do something like that."

I look down at my hands. "I didn't think I would be able to, either. I still don't believe it."

Simone shoots to her feet. "Never mind about that! Let's find out about your schooling. What do you have to do to transfer your credits?"

"I don't know. That's what I have to find out."

"Forget about that, Simone!" Emeline counters. "That's boring! Geneviève doesn't want to work on all that stodgy old paperwork right now."

"What does she want to do?" Simone asks. "Isn't that what we're here for?"

"Of course not!" Emeline exclaims. "We're here to entertain her and keep her occupied. She can work on all of that another time when we aren't here—sometime when she has nothing better to do."

"Then what are we going to do instead?" Simone asks.

Emeline turns to me. "What do *you* want to do today?"

"I don't know. I was just catching up on sleep when you two showed up."

They both burst out laughing like that's the funniest thing ever.

"I know what we can do." Simone grabs the laptop and brings it over to the couch. "We can read all the stories the press is writing about us."

"Yes!" Emeline pumps her fist. "Let's do it!"

"Why is that interesting?" I ask. "Don't we already know the stories the press is writing about us?"

"Not *those* stories!" Emeline tells me. "You're thinking of the mainstream news stories. These are way more interesting."

"I don't understand. If you aren't talking about the mainstream news stories, which stories do you mean?"

Simone shoots her eyes to the couch cushion next to her. "Sit down and learn something, honey. This is going to be an eye-opener for you."

I don't know what I'm getting myself into, but they both grin and giggle so excitedly that my curiosity overcomes my good sense.

I sit down next to Simone while she opens the laptop. Emeline sits on Simone's other side.

Simone logs into a browser and navigates to a certain news page. "Here we go," she begins. "Oh, here's a perfect one. 'Crown Prince Gustav Caught On Camera In Kinky Threesome With Thai Sex Workers.'"

Emeline bursts out in loud laughter. "Priceless!"

I gasp. "Seriously?!"

"Of course not!" Simone fires back. "It's fake news to create drama in the tabloid market. Here's another one. 'Princess Emeline Secret Baby Bombshell—Who's The Father?'"

Emeline practically falls off the couch laughing.

I can't stop staring at the screen. "But....they have pictures! How is that even possible?"

"They're deepfakes," Simone tells me. "They're AI-enhanced and doctored to make them look like us. Some of them even say they have eyewitness accounts. Here's one about you and Christophe. 'Royal Wedding Exposé—Prince Christophe and Princess Geneviève Secret Lovers Before the Wedding.'"

I force myself to look away. "I can't listen to this."

"Don't worry. That's the only one about you. Here's one about me. 'Princess Simone Caught in Raunchy Love Affair With Hired Security Gun.'" Simone laughs. "That actually sounds like something I would do."

"It is not!" Emeline interjects. "Don't lie! You would never do it with one of your security guys. That's just wrong."

Simone's eyes twinkle when she smiles at me. "She's so protective of her big sister."

Emeline bumps her arm. "Read some about the guys."

"Which of the guys do they write about?" I ask.

"All of them except Pascal. They never write anything about him." Simone bends over the screen. "Here's one. 'Prince Renáld Goes On Wild Spring Break Rampage In South Florida.'"

"Wow," I breathe. "I never knew he had it in him."

Emeline explodes in laughter. "He doesn't! That's the joke. Ooo! Look! 'Prince Dorian Arrested For Drunken Assault in Rome.' Now that one I could believe."

"I could believe it if he ever left the palace," Simone adds. "Let's check the dates. Oh, yeah. See? They say the drunken assault happened the night before Christophe's and Geneviève's wedding. He was here all night—and he couldn't have gotten arrested for a drunken assault in Rome and still made it home in time for the wedding."

I lean back on the couch. I don't need to see any more. "Who knew our lives were so interesting?"

Simone shoots me a smirk. "The truth is stranger than fiction, isn't it?"

I find myself smiling back at her. "Yeah, it is. Thanks for coming by, you two. I really needed this."

Emeline swats her sister's shoulder. "So who's the lucky security hunk? Why have you been keeping this hidden from us?"

Simone turns bright red. "I'll let you know as soon as I meet him."

"Do the security guards have any rules against socializing with the Royal Family?" I ask.

"All the servants have strict rules against any kind of fraternization," Simone tells me. "It doesn't matter because I would never get together with one of them anyway."

"The security guards aren't exactly servants, are they?" I ask. "Not that kind, anyway."

"They're on the palace payroll," Simone replies. "That's the only requirement. It doesn't matter if they're a security guard, a chauffeur, mopping the floors, or washing dishes in the kitchen. The same rules apply to everyone."

"Father would castrate the guy anyway," Emeline interjects. "And that's saying nothing about what Christophe and the other guys would do."

Simone throws up her hands. "None of this matters because I'm not getting together with one of the security guys! That's just stupid."

"You have enough rich admirers anyway," Emeline tells her. "You can take your pick. You don't need to have a raunchy affair with one of the servants."

"What makes it a raunchy affair instead of a romantic love connection?" I ask. "What's the difference?"

Both sisters burst out laughing and Simone turns bright red. "The difference is in the wording the press uses to describe it," Simone tells me.

"Then you could just as soon have a raunchy affair with a rich playboy," I point out. "Would the press describe that as a romantic love connection just because the guy has more money?"

"Only because Father might actually consider the rich playboy as a suitable husband for her," Emeline replies.

Simone stands up so fast that she almost drops the laptop. She shuts it and puts it on the coffee table just in time. "That's enough! I'm not listening to this! You two can sit here and come up with all the imaginary stories you want about my raunchy love affairs. I'm done!"

She sails out of the room. Emeline smirks at me and follows her sister. "Have fun with your new laptop," she tells me. "See you around."

Chapter 15: Christophe

I meet up with Geneviève outside the palace dining room. I'm not wearing a tux this time and she isn't wearing an elaborate gown from Lucille's wardrobe.

Geneviève still looks beautiful in a close-fitting dress with a low, pointed, sweetheart neckline and her bare arms exposed. Her outfit still makes her look stately and angelic even though it's understated.

Her skin glows with light and color. She looks a thousand times better than she did this morning when I had to leave her alone to cope with her brother's death.

Her hair falls over her neck, chest, and shoulders in delicate ringlets. I really wish I could sweep her into my arms and kiss her the way I did this morning.

A jet of thrilling excitement rushes to my guts when I remember kissing her. I want to take her further, but I don't dare to. I don't want to hurt or frighten her.

I don't want to do anything she isn't ready for. She's too good for that.

She's been so vulnerable with me. She's so honest and caring even when she's guarded.

I find myself standing way too close to her—close enough to kiss her. "I'm sorry about our dinner date. I thought we would be able to get out of this when I said we would have dinner together, but it's too short notice."

Her cheeks flush. Does she want to kiss me as much as I want to kiss her?

"It's all right," she breathes. "Thank you for sending your sisters over to spend time with me. They were really sweet."

"They better not have corrupted you with any crazy ideas."

She laughs and her eyes sparkle up at me. "It wasn't like that. They were really nice—and thank you for the computer. It was great. It really helped me take my mind off of everything. It was exactly what I needed."

I let my hand slip into hers. "Maybe we could just take some time to spend with each other....when we get back to the apartment.....if you want to. We hardly know each other."

She bursts into a beautiful smile. "I would really like that."

I squeeze her hand, but the dining room doors open behind us just then. I offer her my arm and she smiles at me when she takes it.

She's beautiful—and she's such a good person. I never dreamed she could do everything she's doing for me. I really need to be careful with her.

I don't have a chance to say anything else to her before we walk into the dining room. My whole family is there—but only the family. This is a private dinner just between us.

We make a circuit of the room to greet and talk to everyone. Geneviève knows everyone in my family much better now—or almost everyone.

My sisters both hug her. "You didn't run off to the coast of Patagonia as the love slave of some Antarctic researcher?" Simone asks. "I read that one on the news just a few hours ago."

Geneviève laughs—and it's a genuine laugh for a change. "I think I would remember that."

Simone shoots me a grin. "You better keep an eye on her. She can teleport anywhere in the world, have a wild fling with someone you've never met, and teleport back before morning."

Now I'm the one who laughs. "That would definitely be a useful skill to have."

"Tell Christophe about your boyfriend," Geneviève interjects.

Simone turns bright red and turns away. "I'm not talking to you."

Geneviève laughs when Simone raises her hand and plows off into the crowd.

"She has a boyfriend?" I ask. "Why am I only hearing about this now?"

"It's an inside joke," Geneviève tells me. "She doesn't really."

"Phew!" I exclaim. "I was worried."

We meet up with my brothers next. Both of them kiss Geneviève's hand. "I'm glad you're feeling better," Pascal tells her. "I was worried about you after last night."

She blushes and looks away. "Thank you. Thank you for all your help last night—and thank you, Renáld. I'm forever in your debt."

He waves that away. "It's nothing. I'm just glad you're okay. The security lapse was our fault. It never should have happened."

I change the subject. "Did Chevalier have a coronary when you told him to change the schedule?"

Renáld laughs. "I think he might be drawing up a kill list instead. You know how he feels about anyone changing his schedules."

"Tell him to come talk to me."

"Just take a team of armed security guards with you," Pascal tells me. "Either that or wait a week until all the appointments are past. Then he may have fallen into a depression and he won't be so dangerous."

"Is he really dangerous?" Geneviève asks. "He seemed so nice when I talked to him."

"It's an inside joke," I tell her. "He's just a stickler for his schedules. We joke about him reacting badly when anyone changes anything, but it happens all the time. Sometimes the people who arranged the events change them or cancel them for whatever reason. Then we don't have to go and that throws his schedule off."

"He's used to it," Pascal adds. "He makes it out to be bigger than it is. That's part of the joke. He's in on it and makes a joke out of himself."

"Oh," she murmurs. "I see."

"You'll get to know us all soon," Renáld tells her. "Then all of this will make more sense to you."

"Look out," Pascal murmurs. "Here comes the Tasmanian Devil."

Geneviève tightens her grip on my arm and moves a few inches closer to me when Dorian, Casim, and Salvatore come over to join us.

Dorian elbows me. "Did you hear about New Zealand defeating Ireland in the Rugby World Cup? There will be blood on the streets of Dublin tonight."

"No one can defeat New Zealand," Renáld tells him. "They're going all the way to the top this year. You mark my words."

"What about France?" Geneviève asks.

The guys sneer at her. "Silence, peon," Salvatore snaps. "Blasphemer."

She laughs. "Don't listen to him," Pascal chimes in. "France is already out of the match. We fell on our asses in the worst possible way. We embarrassed ourselves."

"Heresy!" Salvatore howls. He turns in different directions to call over the noise of all these talking voices. "Sacrilege!"

"Our team isn't even good enough to play New Zealand," Renáld adds. "We never stood a chance."

Geneviève leans closer to me and murmurs in my ear. "I think your parents are trying to get our attention."

I glance down the hall. My parents stand near the head of the table talking to my aunt Marguerite and my cousin Daphne.

My father nods at me and my mother waves for me and Geneviève to go over there.

I excuse myself from my brothers and cousins. At least Geneviève doesn't have to worry about the guys holding anything against her.

My parents both hug Geneviève, too. "You look stunning, my dear," my father tells her.

"Thank you, Your Highness," she murmurs. "Your family has been taking extra good care of me."

"I'm glad to hear it. You only have to ask if you need anything at all. We're all at your service."

She looks away. She knows what that means. The people who know what she did last night all admire her. They're all unbelievably grateful to her.

Whatever problems we might have with her family—none of that applies to her—not anymore. She's as welcome here among us as if she never belonged to any enemy family.

My aunt hugs her next and starts talking to her about the university. "I'm involved in the university trust board," my aunt tells Geneviève.

"If you need any help with admissions or expediting your transfer, I might be able to talk to a few people."

"Thank you," Geneviève exclaims. "I checked the requirements earlier today. I don't think it will be too complicated."

"I also know a few key people in the chemistry department," my aunt tells her. "I would love to introduce you."

"That would be great...." Geneviève glances at me. "I don't know how that would work with the security arrangements."

My aunt waves that away. "Never mind about that. We can arrange for these people to get accidentally invited to an event you're already attending—one you don't have any choice about attending—one that can't be canceled. Then you can meet them there and kill two birds with one stone. See?"

"That sounds amazing!" Geneviève exclaims. "Thank you so much."

"We better sit down and eat," my father interjects. "We can discuss all of this with Chevalier after dinner."

Chapter 16: Geneviève

C hristophe pulls my chair out for me to sit down at the grand palace dining table. Our seats are positioned again right next to the Crown Prince and Princess Jasmine.

Christophe sits down at the place next to me—between me and his father. This dinner feels so different from the last one.

I know his whole family now. Some I know better than others. I don't know Johanne and Daphne very well. I don't know Christophe's three male cousins very well, either.

At least I feel like I could know them well. They don't hate me anymore.

His brothers, sisters, parents, and aunt are all so nice. They really treat me like one of the family now.

I guess I am one, now that I'm married to Christophe.

Sitting down to dinner with them feels like sitting down to dinner with any other family. They don't act like royalty at all when they're behind closed doors with just each other.

The fancy dining room and expensive dishes don't dampen the feeling that these are all just normal people. Christophe's brothers and cousins talk about rugby. His sisters talk about social media drama.

Everyone talks during dinner. The servers and butlers come and go the same way they do at official state dinners, but the atmosphere becomes relaxed and convivial instead of stiff and formal.

"What did you want to talk to me about?" the Crown Prince asks Christophe after a few minutes.

"I think we need to hire a new head of security—a professional, this time. Someone who really knows what he's doing when it comes to guarding heads of state. I don't think we should trust that to me and the guys anymore."

The Crown Prince cocks his head to one side. "That's interesting. What makes you say that?"

"Apart from all the security breaches we've had lately?" Christophe asks. "Isn't that enough?"

"Don't you think you and your brothers and cousins are taking enough precautions?"

"I thought we were, but I was obviously mistaken about that. There are too many things I don't know to look for. That's why we need someone trained and experienced in all of this."

"What about putting security guards inside the grounds?" Prince Gustav asked.

Christophe shrugged. "We can put all the Band-Aids we want on it. We can try to plug all the holes with more and more security guards. We can station security guards in every single one of our bedrooms. None of that will take the place of one person in charge of all of this—someone who actually knows what he's doing and can tell the rest of us what to do. I'm no security expert. None of us is."

Prince Gustav looked down at his plate. "I see your point."

Christophe glances over at me. I realize in that moment that I haven't been eating. I got too focused on their conversation.

I shouldn't have been eavesdropping even though I'm sitting right next to them.

Christophe and Prince Gustav start talking about the steps the Royal Family is taking to scrub their security records and spread the story that Renáld killed Raoul after Raoul broke into the grounds.

Christophe and the Crown Prince never actually mention Raoul by name. They never mention me being involved. They skirt around any details about what really happened.

Other than saying the words out loud, neither of them acts too concerned about talking over their security situation in front of me. Is it possible they don't consider me a security threat anymore?

Maybe this is all an elaborate test. Maybe the Crown Prince and his sons are trying to manipulate me in reverse to see if I take this information back to my family.

I don't know how I would do that when I never leave the palace. I suppose I could email my father or Remi.

I never want to talk to my father or Remi again. I really hope they never find out what really happened to Raoul. I just hope and pray my father and Remi receive and believe the story about Renáld killing Raoul with a tree branch.

The conversation turns pretty soon. Christophe and his father joke about Chevalier, too. Then they talk about the Rugby World Cup. I don't mention France again.

The dinner ends with the usual standing around talking. I stay near Christophe even when we talk to other people. I don't know why he makes me feel so much better—probably because I already know he doesn't hold last night against me.

None of these other people hold it against me, either, but I'm still causing them a security problem in more ways than one.

The evening finally ends when Prince Gustav and Princess Jasmine excuse themselves to go to bed. Everyone else leaves at the same time. We talk to the others outside, but only for a few minutes before the rest of the family splits off to their separate apartments.

Prince Gustav and Princess Jasmine are both long gone by the time Christophe and I head to ours.

"You should probably go to sleep, too," Christophe tells me on the way. "You didn't get much sleep last night."

"I fell asleep in the middle of the day. I took a nap before Simone and Emeline came to visit. I'm not tired." I look up at him. "Are you? You got even less sleep last night than I did."

"I'll be all right. I'm a night owl."

"I'm starting to understand that. Why didn't you go to sleep last night?"

"I just had a lot on my mind. Sometimes I start thinking about things and I can't put it out of my mind—especially when it's something related to palace security. It's a lot of responsibility and the whole family's safety rests on my decisions."

"How did you come to take charge of security anyway?" I ask. "You aren't qualified for that."

"I'm not qualified for any of this. I got pushed into the role when César left—just like everything else. That's why I think we need to hire a new security chief."

"Do you think César is still alive out there somewhere?"

He shrugs. "I don't think it matters anymore. He'll never come back. We'll probably never hear from him or see him again. We'll probably never even find out what happened to him."

"It's such a shame." I look up at him again. "And it's a shame what happened to you. Your life could have been so different."

He shrugs, but he won't look at me. "That's life, I guess. I just have to play the hand I'm dealt. It isn't like Pascal could become Crown Prince if I bailed out."

We get to the apartment just then. He opens the door for me to enter and then shuts the door behind me.

I groan as I start to unzip my dress. "Why do these dresses have to be so uncomfortable?"

He laughs and pulls off his jacket. "At least you don't have to wear a tie."

"I'd like to see you cram yourself into one of these push-up bras. I can barely breathe."

His eyes twinkle at me and follow me into the bedroom where I squirm out of the dress. I lay it on the chair before I change into my pajamas and bathrobe.

I happen to pass the bedroom door and see Christophe sitting on the couch looking at his phone again.

I take the pins out of my hair while I go in there and sit on the other end of the couch from him. "Are you checking the security cameras again?" I ask.

He puts his phone down. "No, I was checking some employment listings for security specialists."

"You don't really plan to hire someone off an employment listing, do you? You need someone more qualified than that."

"I wasn't planning to hire someone off an employment listing. I was just checking the caliber of specialist these listings are advertising for. I need to do some more research before I think about who I want to hire and where I want to hire them from." He turns in my direction. "I don't want you to think about the security situation anymore. That's my job."

"I have to think about it. I am the security situation."

He makes a face. "You're much more than that."

"You know what I mean." I lean forward to put my hair pins in a pile on the table. Then I lean all the way back and curl up at my end of the couch. "Don't tell me you plan to spend all night tonight working on the security situation, too."

"No, not tonight. I want to spend tonight with you."

My head shoots up. "With me?! Why? Do I need a chaperone?"

He bursts into a smirk. "Maybe you do. Come here."

He holds out his arms to me. We've been acting so romantic toward each other lately—or at least he's been acting romantic toward me.

He kissed me this morning and we keep spending the night together. I guess this is the next logical step.

I crawl down the couch and settle into his arms. He scoots down the cushions and leans back so I lie half on top of him with his arms around me and my head resting on his chest.

I sink into him and shut my eyes. This feels so good.

I don't have to worry about anything when I'm with him. All the same problems still loom in the background, but his presence somehow makes them all seem so much farther away.

I might not be able to forget them completely, but I have to believe he'll handle them or that they won't be as threatening as they seem as long as he's here.

He hugs me against himself, kisses my forehead, and strokes his fingers through my hair as we both sink into the couch. He rubs my back.

Everything he does relaxes me. My brain shuts down in deep, peaceful, soft relaxation.

"Are you sure you don't need to get up and go do stuff?" I mumble into his chest.

"No way," he murmurs back. "I don't need to be anywhere but right here."

"I'm sorry I suggested that we do it that first night. I didn't understand. I thought you would want to. I didn't understand that you didn't."

His warm breath enters my brain through my hair. "We had a lot of misunderstandings on both sides then. It's in the past now. I know your value now and I know you're loyal. I would never want to do it with anyone who doesn't actually want me."

"I.....do want to......"

He squeezes me tighter. "This arrangement isn't enough. I would still consider it coercion if that was the only reason. I would only do it if you actually liked me and wanted to be with me for myself. Besides, you're a virgin and I wouldn't want to hurt you."

I open my mouth to say that I do want him. I like him and I want him for himself, but my old mental blocks stop me from saying that.

Am I really ready for that? Will I ever be? I can't answer that even for myself.

That's what he means. How can I do it with him when I'm not even ready to think about doing it with anyone?

I want to say so many things to him. I want to apologize for all of this, but he'll only tell me not to.

I also want to apologize for trapping him in a marriage he doesn't want, but that's his whole life now.

I kick myself for feeling sorry for myself. His life is much worse than mine even though his life isn't really bad at all. He's a prince. He just doesn't want to be one.

Lying like this on the couch with him lulls me into a trance. I must be more exhausted than I think I am.

He smells good. His body feels strong and soft at the same time. I hug him a little closer as we both relax further.

He must be tired, too. His breathing evens out and gets deeper. His arm loosens around my shoulders, but he doesn't let go before he falls asleep.

Knowing he's asleep sends me a little further into total relaxation and I feel myself drifting off. I'm drifting off in Christophe's arms again.

This feels right. It feels like the best place I could possibly be. I don't want to be anywhere else.

Chapter 17: Geneviève

I wake up in the middle of the night with a cramp in my back from lying in the wrong position in bed—except I'm not in bed.

I groan when I peel myself off of Christophe. He squirms, groans, and then snarls when he tries to straighten himself out. He fell asleep in the wrong position, too.

"We should go to bed," I mumble and try to stand up off the couch.

I'm still half asleep and I almost fall over the coffee table. Christophe shoots off the couch in time to catch me. "Be careful," he tells me.

He keeps his hold on me and helps steer me across the shadowy room. I can't see well enough to avoid the furniture.

He guides me into my bedroom and down onto my bed. Then he stands up straight. Is he about to leave?

I don't want him to. I want to sleep with him here the way we have the last two nights. I grab his hand and pull him down to get into bed with me.

I'm tired enough and groggy enough that I feel myself starting to drift off even now. Keeping my eyes open takes too much effort.

He takes a step forward and then lowers himself onto the bed. He's still fully clothed as usual except that he isn't wearing a jacket or a tie. He's just wearing his shirt.

I sink back on my pillows when his weight compresses the mattress next to me. His arms fold around me and he kisses my hair again.

I crawl back into his arms and press my face against his shirt as my hands and arms slide around his waist and ribs. I should go back to sleep, but I get distracted by what he feels and smells like.

His body keeps me just awake enough to sense that I'm touching him through his shirt. I've been holding onto him so much lately, but he feels different now.

He hugs me tighter and then tries to pull the covers up to tuck them around me. He can't bring them as high as he wants to when his weight is lying on top of them.

I open my eyes and try to look around when he gets off the bed enough to pull the covers up. I don't want to let go of him.

I can't see enough in the dark, but it doesn't really work for him to hold me with the covers in the way. In the end, he scoots under them so we can lie right next to each other.

I'm still wearing my pajamas and bathrobe. Neither of us can touch any other part of each other. We both settle down with our arms around each other, but neither of us falls back to sleep. Holding him feels too good—or maybe I already got all the sleep I need.

I wait for him to fall back to sleep, too, but he doesn't. He just lies there. "Are you asleep?" I ask even though I know he isn't.

"Yes," he replies.

I laugh and throw back my head to look at the dark place where his voice is coming from. "So am I. Maybe we're dreaming together."

He turns his head and his voice murmurs from a few inches away from me. His hand comes to rest on my cheek.

He murmurs, "Yes, we are," before his mouth smothers me in his kiss.

Kissing him sends me into a satin blur of heavenly sensations and emotions. I wrap my arms around his neck and let myself melt into the soft warmth of his lips.

He tightens his embrace to pull me against him. That kiss erases all my cares in the blissful feeling that everything will be all right because he's here.

He keeps raking his fingers back through my hair, squeezing the back of my neck, and compressing his hand into my spine while we kiss.

All those touches—none of them escalates—and yet all of them come together to flood me with so much pleasure and sensation. Each one brings my body closer to him and softens all the defenses that would hold us apart.

We're kissing in deep, succulent, passionate kisses. I can't deny that anymore. We're passionate about each other.

All that passion comes through when we kiss. He isn't just comforting me or taking care of me because I'm emotionally distraught. He's really kissing me like that and I'm responding.

I respond beyond my wildest dreams. Kissing him brings up so many forbidden, torrential desires I never knew I had. I want to unleash all my tortured, suppressed lusts on him, but I don't let myself do that.

He's still a stranger even though we're already married.

I don't want him to be a stranger. I want to merge with him in this overpowering kiss.

That kiss keeps building in heat and intensity even though neither of us takes it any further. His body tenses, but my bathrobe gets in the way of me feeling him the way I want to.

My eyes float open in a sea of blissful desire. My body buzzes with energy for him. My flesh starts to ache and throb between my legs. I've never kissed anyone like this with so much blistering passion building between us.

A glimmer of light comes through the patio doors for me to see his eyes. They glisten in the darkness—just enough for me to see him staring back at me.

I catch my breath and that moment releases something else in me. I want him. I want him to take me. I want him to be the one who takes my virginity.

He's my husband. I want to be with him like that. I want him to teach me and carry me to the stars in ways I never let myself go with anyone else. Why not? I'll never find anyone I trust as much as I trust him.

Our lips and tongues mingle in the darkness. His tongue wraps around my soul in a silky sheen of suggestive, sensual goodness.

Does he see in my eyes how much I want him? Does he feel how much my body craves him?

He responds to that question echoing in my mind. He rolls up on top of me and crushes me under his weight while we kiss.

He drives his body down into me so I feel how hard and tense he's getting. He attacks my mouth kissing me harder and more insistently—but he never closes his eyes.

His eyes burn with fevered madness in the dark. He tells me so much with that powerful, unwavering stare.

He screws his hips into me and drives my legs apart. My bathrobe still protects me, but this position releases an unstoppable flood of smoking hot lust. I can't contain it or hold it back anymore.

I moan and sob in delicious ecstasy as he drills his hard spike between my legs. I spread them wider to wrap around his waist.

He pumps in an unmistakable movement that speaks of so many blistering hot waves of pleasure and climax. I'm escalating beyond control, but I don't ever want to stop.

My wetness stings my raw flesh between my legs. My breath catches every time he grinds down on me. I feel my mind spinning and my own desire becoming overwhelming.

I barely understand what's happening to me, but he knows exactly what he's doing. I'm just starting to float off into space when he pulls another sudden move on me without warning.

He widens his knees, scoops me off the bed, and pulls me all the way back as he rears onto his knees. He sits me on his lap straddling him, pulls my robe open, and wraps his arms around me with only my pajamas between me and his clothes.

The robe falls away. Now he can touch me through my pajamas and turn me on so much more than he ever did before.

He devours my mouth in greedy kisses, squeezes his muscular hands all over my body, and burrows into my neck gnawing and mauling me to the limit.

I scream when his scorching hot mouth comes to rest on my neck. He crawls his way down to my collarbone and gropes around my ribs to my breasts.

His breath comes fast and loud and hot when he kneads them through my shirt, but he doesn't try to take my clothes off.

I scream again when he pinches my nipples through the thin fabric. I can't stop my body from riding down on his hardness. My whole being flies out of control on all this intoxicating passion breaking out of me.

Every touch of his hands turns me on. I want him to tear me open and let all this passion come out one way or the other.

I whimper in an agony of desire when he burrows down to my chest and nibbles my nipples through my shirt. He never once tries to take it off.

I'm really starting to hate how safe I am with him. He won't do anything until I'm ready. Am I ready? I've never wanted anything more in my life, but it still scares me to think I might go all the way even with him.

He tears away from my chest, sits up straight, kisses me once, and leans back. His eyes stab me in the guts when he looks at me all smoking hot like that.

His lips shiver every time he takes a breath. His eyes flash with black fire in the night.

He plants one masterful hand on the lowest part of my back and pulls my hips forward into an irresistible rhythm. He guides me to ride down his hard knob until I can't stand it.

"Come on," he husks. "Just like that. Show me how much you want that. Show me how you're gonna love it when I take you just like this."

I can't respond. I scream again as a volcanic jet of fire rushes between my legs. This is what it would feel like if he took me right now—if neither of us was wearing any clothes and I was sitting right there on his naked shaft.

Thinking that snaps my mind the rest of the way out of all reality. We're doing it. I'm riding him while he does it to me.

His hand on my back won't let me stop. I reel in the stratosphere. I can't stop what's about to happen.

He keeps whispering into my face telling me how much I want it. He has no idea how much I want it.

This is how he's going to make me climax when he actually gets around to doing it with me—whenever that turns out to be. He's going to guide me and turn me on until I can't take it anymore and I explode on him.

He doesn't stop until, without warning, he grabs my breast in his other hand. He crushes it in a deep, massaging grip and squeezes my nipple between his thumb and forefinger.

That extra little bit of sensation skyrockets me out of my mind. I scream once and then I can't stop as the tumult of orgasm crashes through me.

I thrash in his arms trying to fight my way through this feeling of flying apart at the seams. I have to keep throwing myself down on him with all my might at the same time. I can't miss out on even one instant of this incredible feeling.

He keeps calling encouragement and filthy hot suggestions about how much I want it. I've never felt anything like this.

Chapter 18: Geneviève

I 'm still convulsing from the cataclysm of straddling Christophe's waist when he eases off, takes hold of my pajama shirt, and peels it off over my head.

I barely notice that he can access my naked breasts now.

He wraps himself around me, inhales them into his mouth, sucks them to drive me wild all over again, and increases the spikes of pleasure shooting through my body.

I try to grab his head, but nothing will stop these cosmic waves of pleasure consuming me beyond all possibilities.

I hold onto him when he leans forward and lays me back down on the bed. He pulls out of my embrace, sits back up on his knees, and draws off my pajama pants and panties.

I can only lie here in a puddle of hazy rapture. I sprawl in front of him completely naked, but even this seems right. My body responds to everything he does—almost as if I was made for him to enjoy.

He leans over me on his hands and knees, kisses me, and works his way down my body, but he doesn't take too long getting there.

He sucks my nipples until I whimper again. He drags his tongue down my stomach and I collapse in an agony of pleasure when he buries his face between my legs.

He left me so raw and sensitive from riding him that the slightest teasing of his tongue spikes me out of this world again.

I writhe in front of him, but he takes hold of me in both hands and moves me where he wants me to go.

He pushes my thighs apart extra wide, raises one of my knees above his head, and attacks me in big, gobbling bites.

I whine and then scream again when I feel him winding me up to another catastrophic orgasm. How is he doing this to me? How does he turn me on so much?

I thrash harder on the bed as my cries escalate, but that only seems to encourage him. He tenses his muscles to hold me down while he takes me to the stars.

I throw my arms above my head trying to find something to hold onto. I see myself stretched out for him, exposed, juicy, succulent, and ready for him to fulfill himself in me.

He doesn't stop. He squeezes my ass in a crushing grip, lifts my swollen flesh into his hungry mouth, and then his fingers dive all the way into me.

I can't stop screaming. I buck my hips against his face as he plunges all the way in. I claw at his arms and grab his hair. I don't know what's happening to me, but he's taking me back there too fast for me to stop it or even think about it.

I scream again and again as the wave breaks. My wetness runs over his face and down my thighs and ass. I feel erotic and unchained in front of him.

I don't even care that he's seeing me in my rawest, most broken state. I need this. I need him in ways I don't even understand.

I careen through so many peaks and valleys that I lose track of everything else. I'm still half out of my mind with all this mind-blowing ecstasy when he grabs me under the armpits and sits me back up on his lap.

"Look at me, baby," he breathes between stolen, panting kisses. "Look at me. See me."

My drunken eyes float open. He hovers in front of me like some kind of otherworldly force of nature.

I sob in deepest soul need when I stare into his eyes. I don't even understand everything I'm feeling for him right now.

He grabs my body all over the way he did before. He grips my bare thighs, squeezes my ass to pull me against him, and his fingers slip a little lower toward the slit of wetness between my legs.

I moan in agony. I don't know what's happening to me, but I can never be the same after this.

He brings his hand around to the front, thrusts it between my legs where I straddle his pants, and presses his flat fingers against my tortured flesh to rub me to the ends of the earth.

I let out another broken scream when I feel him preparing me for another orgasm. Can I survive that? I'm not so sure.

I can't break away from looking into his eyes. Does he see all the aching desire pouring out of my heart right now? Does he even realize how much I need him?

I need so much more than his body. I need so much more than for him to satisfy my body.

I need his heart. I need his care. I need him near me so I always feel like everything is going to be all right.

I want to cry right now because of the way I feel about him. Will he ever feel that way about me? Is there even a chance?

He keeps circling and watching me crumble before his eyes. I pray he can see it because I would never be able to explain it in words.

"Feel me," he murmurs. "Feel me....."

"Christophe....." I choke.

He inches his fingers just a little closer to my aching channel. I need him inside me like I need air to breathe.

"You feel me inside you, don't you?" He dabbles his fingers right there in the gushing fount of wetness. "You need me in there, don't you?"

I scream again when he slips his fingers just a few inches in. My brain doesn't function well enough to answer.

He spirals his fingers around and around in maddening circles as he winds his way inside. I can only sit here, thrash in his arms, and scream as the intensity builds to another earth-shattering climax.

He pulls my hips down on his fingers and drills all the way to my deepest core. He grinds his pelvis up against his hand to impale me on his fingers exactly the way he would if he was doing it to me for real.

"Feel me....." he whispers. "Feel me inside you....."

I can't stop screaming. I can't hold myself up.

He guides me in his arms until I explode into another uncontrollable torrent of bucking and grinding on his hand.

He steers my hips into a deep, thumping, bone-crushing rhythm that never stops. How is he doing this to me? How is he taking me so thoroughly when he isn't even doing anything?

I'm still a virgin. That's what this means. He isn't doing it with me. He never crosses that line. He never even takes his shirt off.

I collapse whimpering and twitching on his shoulder. I can't even lift my arms to hold onto him. He has to do that for me.

He positions my arms around his neck and draws me into a deep, warm hug while the last sobs and quaking eruptions of pleasure and brutal ecstasy pour out of my body.

He slithers his fingers out of me and holds me close while he lies all the way down on top of me on the bed.

His weight comes to rest on me the way it did before. He kisses me a few times, but mostly he just holds me and lets me cling to him for dear life.

I need him to protect me from what just happened. I need him to protect me from how much I need him.

He's my only safety from this. He's the one who will take me there and bring me back. He's the one I'll curl up with after this is over. I'll fall asleep in his arms.

He eventually rolls off me and lies down next to me on the bed with our arms still wrapped around each other. He doesn't do anything until I completely settle down.

I'm just fading off into unconsciousness when he leans back just a little bit. My eyes drift open enough for me to see him looking down at me with all that old fire.

He gave me so much pleasure tonight. I never thought I could ever feel anything like that.

I stare up into his eyes. What is he thinking right now? Is he wishing he could go all the way with me? Is he deciding that he never will? I don't know if I can live with that.

He pulls away just enough to take one of my hands away from around his neck. He guides my arm by the wrist and kisses the palm of my hand.

I don't know what he's doing until he locks his eyes on me with unbelievable power and lowers my hand to the bulge in his pants.

He's harder and hotter now than when he started. He only touches my hand to his fly before he lets go of my wrist. He leaves me to do what I think is best.

I don't have to do it, but I want to. I want to give him something—some little hint of the satisfaction he's been giving me.

His eyes go hard when I pull my arms away from his neck. He never breaks eye contact, but I see him fighting his own overpowering need. He's been holding back all this time because he wants to protect me. He wants to protect me from himself.

He would never hurt me. He doesn't even have to say those words out loud. He would keep holding himself back forever if I needed him to.

I don't want him to. I want him to enjoy tonight as much as I did.

I make sure to work extra slowly when I pull his belt loose. He shudders and his nostrils flare when I accidentally brush his hard shaft buried under his clothes. He's close to the breaking point.

He went through all of that without ever once satisfying himself. He could have. He could have given me one orgasm or none at all.

My heart aches when I see how far he'll go to take care of me. I savor every spasm in his features when I slide his zipper down.

He doesn't let me go any further by myself. I don't know what I'll do with him, but he doesn't give me a chance.

He takes hold of my wrist and pushes my hand down into his shorts. My fingers close around his hot, thick, veiny shaft.

He spasms in my hand. I tremble at the raw masculine power of that rod of iron flesh in my hand. Will I ever be able to face that?

He doesn't give me a chance to decide about that, either. He leans forward just enough to push himself into my hand. He wraps his arms around me, buries his eyes in my neck, and pumps in deep and hard and excruciatingly slowly.

His breath strains and then spikes to a hiss through gritted teeth as he picks up his rhythm. He thrusts deep into my hand escalating in power but not in speed.

He crushes me in a death grip as he arches all the way in, jolts, and then convulses all over as his body releases. He spasms again and again before he collapses in my arms with a broken sigh.

I kiss the side of his head. My heart cracks with so much emotion for him. I just want him to feel some of the pleasure and acceptance that he gave me tonight. I wish I could give him more.

He wilts and his whole body goes limp, but he doesn't relax his hold on me. If anything, he holds me tighter, now that he finally unlocked some of the tension in his muscles.

Sweat soaks through his shirt. He doesn't try to stop me from pulling my hand out of his shorts. He makes no move to take his clothes off or do anything else.

He holds me for a long time as his breathing evens out. He relaxes more and more. We're both on our way to falling back to sleep.

I settle down in his arms. I'm tired after all that exhausting sex.

We did have sex even if we didn't go all the way. We might as well have.

He finally rolls off onto his back and pulls me into his chest. I've been sleeping here for the last few nights, but now I'm naked.

That's the only difference—apart from this deep feeling of satisfaction, relaxation, and contentment that I'm with him. He fulfills me in unimaginable ways. He gave me the greatest night of my life without taking my virginity.

Now I want more than ever for him to be the one to take it. I want to give him that, but I also want to give it to myself. He would be the ultimate gift I could give myself—if I loved him and he loved me as a real married couple.

I don't know if that would ever be possible after everything that's happened between us, but I want that. I've never wanted anything more in my life.

Chapter 19:
Geneviève

I wake up alone again the next morning, but I understand why when I see the clock on the bedside table. It's already almost ten o'clock in the morning. Christophe must have slipped out and left me to sleep.

I'm really going to have to take steps to make sure he gets enough sleep. This can't continue. He'll ruin his health if he doesn't sleep sometime.

I get out of bed, take a shower, and get dressed. I find breakfast waiting for me out in the living room. I'm in the middle of eating it when Antoinette shows up alone this time.

"Where's Chevalier?" I ask.

"He doesn't need to be here for this. He has enough to do organizing the Crown Prince's schedule—now that the rest of you are curtailing your activities."

"Why are you here if we're curtailing our activities?"

She smirks at me. "You have a public gala to attend today. Christophe and the others tried to cancel or reschedule the whole family's public appearances, but no one could cancel everything. The whole family is attending this gala. I'm sure security will be through the roof."

I look down at my plate. "That explains why Christophe left early this morning."

"We'll go down and see Lucille as soon as you finish breakfast."

I don't ask any more questions. I'm getting used to this.

I finish eating, put all my dishes on the service cart, wheel it out of the room, and Antoinette and I head down the corridor to Lucille's fitting room.

We go through the whole procedure in silence this time except when Lucille or one of her people needs to tell me what to do.

She doesn't give me any cheery introductions or tell me how exciting and fun this is going to be. This is all business as usual now.

The gown I'm supposed to wear tonight is a sheer, floor-length, flowing dress of pale beige with a deeply plunging neckline and cap sleeves. It's a stunningly beautiful dress, but even these magnificent gowns don't thrill me the way they used to.

Christophe is right. This is like a job. Wearing costumes is part of the job. I go through the whole process mechanically. I no longer feel like I'm doing anything unusual. This is just part of the job.

I get a surprise when Lucille's attendants put the dress on me and she starts adjusting the bodice, neckline, and side seams.

"What's wrong with this dress?" I ask. "The top feels extra stiff."

"It has a layer of Kevlar stitched into the facing," Lucille tells me around a mouthful of pins.

My eyes fall out of their sockets. "Kevlar? In a ballgown?"

She shoots me a hard look. "Christophe wanted to change your outfit at the last second. He wanted you to wear a short blazer so you could fit a bulletproof vest underneath it, but Chevalier insisted that you wear this instead—so we compromised by including these Kevlar panels in the facing layers." She shrugs. "It's the best we can do at such short notice."

I shut my mouth with difficulty. I never imagined I would be wearing a Kevlar-reinforced ballgown to a charity gala.

I guess anything is possible after everything else that has been going on. It's too late to change it now—and the dress fits perfectly well even with the reinforcing layers.

I sit through hours of hair and makeup styling. Then I have to get a fresh manicure even though I just got one two days ago. Everything has to be perfect.

The makeup artists are just putting the final touches on my face when Simone comes in. She sits in a chair next to mine and the makeup artists start doing her next.

"What's this gala about?" I ask.

"It's a charity ball for the Prince Albert II Foundation. It's an organization that promotes planetary health worldwide. It's one of Father's pet charities. We attend every year."

I nod and face front. "That sounds interesting."

"The security measures are going to be insane."

"That's what Antoinette said. She said Christophe and the other guys wouldn't let us go at all if they could have found a way to cancel the gala."

She makes a face. "I think Father was the one who insisted that we go. It's a family tradition."

My makeup artist finishes just then and tell me I can go back to Lucille's fitting room.

I get too preoccupied with changing my clothes and having Lucille make last-minute adjustments to my dress. I don't have time to talk to anyone or think about anything before it's time to leave.

Three security guards show up to escort me to my limo even though I'm still inside the palace. They show me back to the same covered driveway where Christophe and I came home from the wedding reception.

This is the first time I've left the palace since Christophe and I got married. So much has been happened since then. That day seems like decades ago.

Two of the security guards pivot outward to survey the surroundings while the third opens my door for me. I have to lift my skirts to stop my gown from hitting the pavement.

I slip into the seat and find Christophe already in there. He shoots me a wild grin. "Hello there!"

I can't help grinning back at him. "Hello. I didn't think I would see you before I got to the gala. I thought you would be up to your eye sockets in all the security measures."

"That's what I've been doing since seven o'clock this morning. This gala is turning out to be more trouble than it's worth."

"Simone made it sound like you couldn't talk your father out of it."

"I didn't even try." He slips his arm around my waist and pulls me in close. "Do you think I would get into trouble if I kissed you right now and smudged your lipstick?"

"You probably wouldn't get into trouble for that, but you might get into trouble if you walked into the gala with lipstick on your mouth."

He laughs and kisses my hand instead. "I'll just have to make up for it when we get home."

I blush at him and the limo pulls away from the palace. I don't know where we're going. I don't really care.

He laces his fingers into mine and squeezes. "Stay near me tonight, okay? Don't wander off."

I nod. "Definitely."

I catch him giving me a deep, searching look. Is he thinking about last night as much as I am?

We show up at the venue pretty soon. Security guards surround the door even before they open it.

The limo has to pull up in front of the venue on the main street. Hundreds of people and reporters crowd outside. The security guards have to flank us on both sides to stop everyone from shoving and trying to get near us.

Christophe keeps a tight hold on my hand and leads me inside. We don't look right or left or talk to anyone until the security guards escort us into the venue.

More security guys surround us even then. They don't leave us alone for an instant.

Christophe and I enter the crowd. The hall is packed with people all dressed up in elegant eveningwear. I don't see anyone I know, but we meet up with the rest of the Royal Family pretty soon.

Security forms a ring around the Crown Prince and Princess Jasmine even when they're talking to ordinary people.

The security guards keep glancing everywhere, searching every face, and the guards get tense and annoyed every time someone puts their hand in their pocket.

I stick close to Christophe the whole time. A few people come up to me to congratulate me on my wedding or to talk to Christophe, but this doesn't happen very often.

The gala starts pretty soon and the Royal Family retires to their box in the upper gallery for the speeches and announcements from the charity organizers.

The security guards stand outside our box. They don't need to come inside it, but I spot more security guards on the opposite side of the hall. Some of those men even have rifles with scopes trained on the surrounding stands and the people on the main event floor.

The security personnel distract me from paying attention to the speeches and dedications. The ceremony goes on for a long time. Then we have to attend the reception afterward.

Christophe and I stay together through the whole thing almost until the very end. I'm just counting down the minutes before we can leave before one of the security men comes over and whispers in Christophe's ear.

"I have to go take care of something," he tells me. "Don't go anywhere. I'll be right back. These guys will be with you the whole time."

I nod and squeeze his hand before he hurries away. He must have to go deal with some security matter.

He's right that it doesn't really work to have the Royal Family handling their own security. They need experts to handle that for them.

I'm just wondering what to do with myself until he comes back when an older lady comes over to me, seizes my hand, and presses it between both of hers.

"I'm so happy for you, my dear!" she quavers. "You don't know how happy we all are that the Crown Prince will finally have grandchildren who can inherit the throne after him."

"Um....thank you," I reply. "I'll try to do my best for the Royal Family."

"We were all so pleased when Prince Christophe got married!" she gushes. "We couldn't be happier! You're the perfect choice for him."

I don't tell her there was no choice involved. I just say, "Thank you," again.

She beams at me and presses my hand again. She doesn't look like she's in any danger of letting go anytime soon.

The security guys move in to send her on her way, but she leaves before they can intervene. I look around for Christophe and see him talking to another, older man across the reception.

He catches my eye and gives me a small nod. At least he can see me in case anything happens.

I feel too exposed all of a sudden. I really wish I *was* wearing a bulletproof vest right now even though no one here is threatening me.

I consider turning around and walking over there to stand next to Christophe. Maybe he doesn't want that. Maybe he's in the middle of a private conversation he doesn't want me to hear.

Just then, another old lady comes over to me. She hunches over and hobbles on a walking stick. She has to crane her neck to look up at me.

I hold out my hand to shake hers. Here we go again.

I jump in surprise when she grabs my hand. Her hand isn't frail and bony like the last old lady. This hand is thick, meaty, muscular, and strong.

I stare down at the hand holding onto mine. The skin is smooth and clear. It's a man's hand.

My eyes shoot up, but the old woman is already leaning in close and telling me in an identical squeaky, scratchy voice how happy she is that I married Christophe.

That's the moment when I recognize the eyes staring back at me. The woman—or whatever she is—leans in extra close and lowers her voice to a deep, chesty whisper. It's a man's voice.

"Don't give anything away," he breathes. "I'm in disguise."

I open my mouth in shock. "Um....Marcel? Is that you?"

"This was the only way I could get near you. The Royal Family's security won't let anyone near the palace anymore."

"What are you doing here?" I exclaim.

"I came to see you." He switches back into his little-old-lady voice and pipes on and on about how beautiful and lucky I am and how proud the whole country is of me.

Then he switches back to his masculine undertone. I still can't believe I'm actually talking to my own brother like this.

"Something happened to Raoul," he murmurs. "We don't know what it was, but we think the Royal Family knocked him off somehow. Then they concocted that stupid story about him breaking into the palace grounds. They probably hired a hit team to take out Raoul—but that isn't why I came. Are you okay? Is anyone hurting you? We can get you out of there if we have to."

"I'm....I'm fine. No one is doing anything to me."

He shakes himself like he has to force himself to pay attention. He breaks into his little-old-lady act for a couple more minutes before he whispers under his breath. "Listen to me, sweetie. This is important. We're going to retaliate against the Royal Family in four days. They're taking a security convoy to the Château des Gennennois, their country estate south of Nice."

"What do you mean....you're going to retaliate?" I don't want to know.

"We're going to hit the convoy. They always move around from one residence to another, especially when they have security concerns about one location. The convoy is the only place where we can hit the Crown Prince and all his sons at the same time. The Royal Family will never recover and the monarchy might even come to an end. We even have plans in motion to track down César and get rid of him, too."

I can only stand and stare at the person in front of me. Is this really my brother?

Marcel has always been the calmest, friendliest, and the most easy-going of my brothers. Is he really talking about carrying out a murderous hit on the Royal Family—for what?

I could believe it of Remi or Raoul, but not Marcel. Will my family even be able to find César? None of the international law enforcement agencies on the planet can find him. What chance do my father and brothers have?

Marcel doesn't notice my hesitation.

"Now listen to me," he murmurs. "This is important. You need to make sure you position yourself in the third limo in the convoy or you might get killed in the initial assault. The hit team will strike where Avenue Andre Theuriet intersects La Provençale highway near Fort de la Drête. As soon as the limo comes to a stop, you need to get out of the car and get as far away from the convoy as you can. The hit team will be keeping an eye out for you to make sure you get out in time and then to get you to safety before they finish off the last car. Do you understand all of that?"

I can only nod in stunned disbelief. He's really serious about this.

I don't have to ask what he means by "finish off the last car". I'll be riding with Christophe at least. Some other members of the Royal Family might be in the same car with me.

That's what Marcel means by "finishing them off". The hit team will move in as soon as I get out of the way. Then they'll kill Christophe, which is what my family wanted me to do in the first place.

How in the hell did I ever get involved in this?

The security guys stand around giving Marcel strange looks. The guards can't figure out why I'm carrying on this murmured conversation with what looks like an old lady.

Marcel gives me one pointed look and slips away into the crowd with those words ringing in my head. My family will carry out a mass hit on the Crown Prince, Princess Jasmine, and all their children.

I have four days. Now what am I going to do?

Chapter 20: Christophe

I nod, shake hands with the secretary of the Prince Albert II Foundation, and he strides away into the crowd.

I turn around to go rejoin Geneviève only to discover her coming straight toward me. She glides on a pillow air as she crosses the room. Her exquisite gown flows all around her sultry body.

No one understands that body better than I do. I can't wait to get her back to my apartment where I can get my hands on her.

I don't care if I ever go all the way with her. I don't have to. I can enjoy all her delights exactly the way she is now.

Part of me wants to preserve her virginity forever. I want to cherish it like the delicate flower that it is.

I won't be able to have children with her if I do that—and what's the point of us being married if we don't have children?

I'm my father's heir. I have to have children and that means taking her virginity....sometime. I won't do it now. I don't know when I'll do it, but it won't be now. She's too beautiful and priceless the way she is.

All those thoughts cross my mind as she slithers across the floor to meet up with me. She smiles at me as she slips her hand into my elbow......but there's something wrong with that smile. I don't know what it is, but her smile looks fake.

I've been seeing too many fake smiles from her recently. I don't want to see any more. I peer down into her eyes searching for the answer. "Are you okay?" I ask.

She nods and her eyes sparkle with some other kind of mystery. "I'm fine. Did you take care of your business?"

"It's all taken care of." I stop talking to her to shake hands with someone. Then the same person shakes hands with her, congratulates her, and kisses her hand before the person leaves. I can't even remember who the person is.

I want to turn back to her, but just then, one of the foundation officers climbs up onto a podium to give a toast to the Crown Prince. Then the guy launches into a speech.

Geneviève squeezes my arm tighter, inches closer to me, and clings to me. I just happen to glance down at her before she casts a terrified look around her at the surrounding people.

Now I know something is wrong. She barely smiles at all except when more people come up to us to introduce themselves and congratulate us.

Her smile drains the minute those people walk away. Now she's back to acting petrified and watchful the way she acted when she brought the gun into the palace.

I don't know what to make of it, but I can't ask her about it here. I can see perfectly well that she isn't fine or okay or whatever other meaningless catchphrase she would use if I asked her again.

I just have to wait until we get somewhere more private. My father finally takes his leave. He and my mother get into their limo. The security guys escort me and Geneviève to ours.

"What's going on with you?" I ask as soon as they shut the doors with both of us in the car.

She squirms on the seat and looks out the window. She won't even look in my general direction to make eye contact with me. "I need to talk to you about something. It's important—but I have to wait until we get somewhere private."

"We're in private here. No one can hear us. Why can't you tell me now?"

She shakes her head. She still won't meet my eye. "I can't tell you here! I have to wait until we get home to the apartment."

I stare at her trying to figure out what could be that important. I want to know what it is now, but it must be too important for that.

I can't think what would be that important unless it has something to do with what we did last night. Maybe she regrets it and wants to keep our relationship simply as a business arrangement.

Don't ask me what I'll do if that happens. I'm really starting to care about her—like she really might be my wife.

I always knew I would get married and have a family someday. It's part of the job.

I never put too much thought into the question of who I would marry. Now that I actually am married, I can't think of anyone I would rather be married to.

I already know Geneviève. I know she's a good person and I know she and I get along. We have chemistry and I know she's dedicated to me and the Royal Family. I don't see how it can get any better than that.

I don't want to let her go. I definitely don't want to go back to this just being an arrangement. That would be my worst nightmare.

She won't stop fidgeting on the seat over there. She won't look at me no matter what. She keeps her head turned to look out the window the whole way back to the palace.

I take a chance, swivel over to the seat next to her, and slip my hand into hers. I squeeze and she squeezes back.

She casts one split-second glance in my direction before she immediately looks away. "I'm sorry I can't tell you now. I'm going crazy."

"It's all right." I have to keep my voice under control. "We'll deal with it together just like we dealt with everything else. I can wait if it makes you feel better."

"I just....." She looks out the window and her voice cracks. "I don't know what to do!"

I tighten my grip on her hand. "You're going to tell me whatever is bothering you. Did something happen at the gala?"

She nods down at her other hand resting on the seat.

"Then you'll tell me when we get back to the apartment. I'm sure a few more minutes won't make that much difference."

We don't talk the rest of the way to the palace. I don't let go of her hand and she doesn't let go of mine. At least now I know this isn't about us.

Something happened at the gala after we got separated. I never should have left her alone. My gut told me not to, but I had to answer the call of duty.

Whatever it was must have happened in those few minutes. Now she's in turmoil again.

When will it ever end? Will it always be like this from now on?

I would do anything to give her some rest and reassurance, but I can't do that when I don't know what's bothering her.

We pass a few casual pleasantries with the rest of the family when we get back. Then Geneviève gives them all the fakest smile in history before we head off to our apartment.

I feel her hand shaking in mine on the way down the corridor. Cold sweat breaks out on her palms. Wow. This is not good at all.

Chapter 21: Christophe

I lead Geneviève into the apartment and shut the door behind me, but she shoves past me and locks it, too.

"Hey!" I murmur. "Take it easy!"

"Marcel was at the gala, Christophe!" she blurts out and starts pacing back and forth with her hand pressed to her forehead. "He came up to me at the gala while you were off doing whatever it was. He came in disguise because the gala was the only place he could talk to me."

My blood runs cold when I hear this. Her brother confronted her at the gala. That's bad. It's another inexcusable security breach.

Marcel always seemed like the most level-headed of Silvain Lefebvre's sons. I always thought Marcel might actually have a brain.

I must have been wrong. Geneviève wouldn't be so agitated about seeing him if he just stopped by to wish her well.

"My family plans to carry out a hit on the Royal Family!" she practically shrieks. She keeps choking on the words while she rushes to pour out the whole story. "He says they're going to assault the convoy of limos on the way to Château des Gennennois in four days! He told me exactly where the hit will take place. He says I have to be in a certain car so I can get out and the team can get me to safety before they finish off the rest of you! My family thinks you carried out a hit on Raoul first! My father and brothers don't believe that Raoul broke into the grounds at all. They think the whole story is false and now my family thinks they have to retaliate!"

I shake myself back to my senses. This is much worse than I feared, but I have to be careful about how I respond.

I hold out my hand to her. "Okay....."

"You don't understand!" She spins around and bellows at me in hysterical panic. "This could be a set-up—of me! They might already know about Raoul and now they're testing my loyalty to see if I tell you! Don't you get it? They could be maneuvering me into a trap and planning to kill me!"

"Okay. Take it easy," I murmur and take another step closer. "We'll work it out. I promise." I put my arms around her, but she keeps trying to push me away and break out of my arms at the same time. "Easy," I breathe. "We have no reason to think they know about Raoul. You said they don't even believe he came onto the grounds, so there's no way your father and brothers could have found out what really happened."

She chokes in my arms. "How am I supposed to believe that?!"

"Okay. Just take it easy." I kiss her hair. God, it must have cost her everything to tell me this. "We'll deal with it."

"How?!" she blurts out. "He told me which car I should ride in so the hit team doesn't kill me when they blow up the convoy, but that could have been a lie. Marcel could have told me to ride in that car so they would be sure to kill me first when they blow up the convoy."

I can't listen to this. "We aren't talking like that or even thinking like that. No one is going to die in the convoy. Now come over here and sit down."

I take her hand, lead her to the couch, and pull her to sit down next to me. I take out my phone and tap on it for a second before I put it away. She needs me more than anything or anyone else right now.

"Now tell me exactly what Marcel said," I tell her.

"I just did," she snaps, but she isn't mad at me. She's more terrified than anything. "He said for me to get as far away from the car as possible after the hit team brings the convoy to a halt. Then they'll take me to safety and move in to finish off anyone left alive."

I nod at nothing. "Then that proves it, doesn't it?"

Her head snaps around. "That proves what?"

"It proves your father and brothers really are trying to save you. They aren't trying to kill you."

"How do you know that? Marcel could have lied about which car to take."

"Baby....listen to me. If they really wanted to kill you, they wouldn't have told you anything about the hit. Marcel could have gotten arrested and maybe even a life prison sentence for trying to evade the security guards at the gala. He risked a lot to tell you which car to ride in. If they really wanted to kill you, he wouldn't have come to the gala at all. They would just blow every car in the convoy. They wouldn't care which car you were in."

She blinks at me and then stares off into space. "Oh. I didn't think of that."

I squeeze her hand. "We'll handle it. You warned us in time. Now our security people can keep an eye on the convoy and make sure they're ready for the hit. Where did Marcel say the hit team would strike?"

"He said they'll strike where Avenue Andre Theuriet intersects La Provençale highway near Fort de la Drête."

I nod again, but my mind is already a million miles away. I have to drag my attention back to the present so I can focus on Geneviève. "I know where it is. That makes sense. The team can strike from the trees and hills on either side of the highway."

"What are you going to do about this?" she demands. "How can you be so casual about someone sending out a hit team to wipe out your whole family? Marcel even said the family is tracking down César to kill him, too."

I have to stop myself from laughing, but it sneaks out anyway. "I'm sorry! I know it isn't funny." I break down laughing again. "I'm sorry!"

"How can you laugh about someone trying to kill your brother—and your parents—and your sisters?!"

"I'm sorry, baby. I'm not laughing about that. I really wish your family could find César. Maybe we should send some of our own people to follow them. They could show us where César is."

She glares at me. I have to fight my facial features under control to take this seriously.

"I'm sorry," I tell her. "I just reacted to what you said."

She compresses her lips, but someone interrupts us by knocking on the door right then. I stand up to answer it and one of the kitchen servers wheels in a service cart with some snacks, sandwiches, and nibbles on it.

I thank the guy and shut the door behind him. I don't lock it this time.

"Come sit down and eat something," I tell Geneviève.

"Aren't you going to go deal with this? You aren't really going to sit down and eat at a time like this, are you?"

"I'm dealing with something more important."

I take her hand and lead her to the table. She drags her feet and stares at the food when I put it in front of her.

I sit across from her and take a bite of my sandwich. She blinks at her plate, at me, and then glances around the room. Her mind is totally gone.

"Did you get to talk to anyone else at the gala who interested you?" I ask.

She whips around extra fast and jumps out of her skin. "Huh?"

"My aunt Marguerite said she would invite some people from the university to meet you at the gala. Did you get to talk to any of them?"

She stares at me and opens and closes her mouth for a second. She doesn't even see the food in front of her.

"Aren't you hungry?" I ask. "You haven't eaten since lunch, have you?"

She takes way too long to look at her plate. She doesn't touch anything. She just looks up at me. "How can you just sit here when this is going on?"

"Is it really bothering you that much?"

"Yes!" she exclaims. "Are you seriously telling me it doesn't bother *you*?"

"What bothers me is how upset you are about it. I'm more worried about you."

"But....your whole family could be in danger."

"My whole family has a team of security agents already working on this. You don't have a team of mental health experts to reassure you and calm you down. I'm the only person who knows about this, so I have to stay here and take care of you."

"I don't want you to take care of me—not if it means putting your family in danger."

"I'm not putting my family in danger by spending a little extra time to help you calm down. Anyway, you're a part of my family now and you're in as much danger as we are if not more."

She looks away and stares down at her hands in her lap. She sits on the edge of her chair.

"You won't be able to calm down until I go deal with it, will you?" I already know it's true, so I wipe my mouth on my napkin and stand up. "All right. I'll go."

She wilts in relief and stands up to meet me. "Thank you so much! I don't know what to do about this....."

"I'll tell you what to do. Go to your room. Take off that dress, get into your pajamas, and go to bed—or maybe eat something first. Don't wait up for me. I'll see you when you wake up."

I kiss her on the forehead. I would like to give her a full, passionate kiss on the mouth and maybe conquer her body right now while she's wearing that dress, but that will have to wait.

Chapter 22: Geneviève

I jolt upright on the couch when the apartment door opens. I freeze when Christophe comes in. He's been gone all night dealing with the threat of my family hitting the convoy when the Royal Family leaves Monaco.

"What's going on?!" I demand. "Where have you been?"

"I've been right downstairs in the security office like I told you I would be." He shuts the door, tears off his jacket, and sits down at the table to eat the food left over from last night. I haven't been able to eat any of it.

I crashed after he left last night. I haven't been able to calm down since I woke up this morning. Now it's nine o'clock in the morning. He's been out there all night.

"What's happening?!" I blurt out. "What are you doing about this?"

"I already told you that," he replies over his shoulder. "The security team will sweep the area before the convoy goes through. Our security people will find the hit team and neutralize them before we pass that section of highway. It's simple now that we know when and where it's going to happen."

"But....what if the whole story turns out to be false? What if this is an ambush, but it's a completely different ambush from the one Marcel said it was?"

He shrugs. "We can only take precautions. I told you we'll deal with it and we will."

"I want to know what the security team is doing. I want to know how they're handling it."

He snorts at me and stuffs another sandwich into his mouth. "That would be a terrible idea. You are NOT getting involved in this. You're already a nervous wreck."

He comes over to the couch, swallows the food in his mouth, and sits down next to me. "I don't want you to worry about this anymore. We're already doing everything possible to contain the situation and protect everyone involved, including you. You wouldn't be able to improve things by sticking your oar in."

I can't look at him. He's right.

I would only wear my nerves to a frazzle if I found out what the security team was doing. I would become obsessed with seeing every foreseeable detail in advance—I mean more obsessed with it than I already am.

He gets my attention by taking my hand and squeezing it in my lap. "We need to find a way to take your mind off of it," he tells me. "You've been dwelling on it too much already."

"How can I take my mind off it when I don't have anything else to do but sit here and think about it?"

He smiles, but he stops himself from laughing. He leans back on the couch and pulls me toward him. "Come here. I didn't get to spend any time with you last night."

He steers me down on top of him on the couch. I rest my head on his chest and he puts his arm around my shoulders.

I wish his presence could calm me down the way it usually does. I wish I could believe him that everything is under control.

This situation is so much worse than Raoul breaking into the palace. Now multiple people are involved. My father and my whole family are involved.

They're planning to kill dozens of people in one hit—and not just dozens of people. My family is planning to kill royalty. What the holy hell is the world coming to where that's even possible?

Christophe presses his lips against my hair and squeezes me tighter. "I want to ask you a question."

I stiffen. "Okay."

"I want to know if you regret what we did the other night—any of it."

My head shoots up and I stare at him from inches away. "Of course not! Why would you ask that? Of course I don't regret it!"

"I just want to be sure. Did you enjoy it?"

"Of course I enjoyed it?!" I fire back. "Couldn't you tell?"

"You might have enjoyed in the moment and regretted it after the fact."

"I don't regret it." I frown at him. "Do you?"

"Not at all." He rears off the couch and gives me one quick peck on the lips. "I just don't know how far to go with you."

I open my mouth to answer and stop myself. I don't know how far I want him to go with me. I don't know much of anything when it comes to him. I want him to and yet I don't want him to.

He watches me and then looks away. "It's all right. We don't have to."

"I want to!" I blurt out. "I told you that."

"You want to what?" He searches deep into my eyes to the bottom of my soul. I already know what he's asking.

He raises both hands, surrounds my face in his warmth, and pulls me down into his mouth. His lips blast my mind full of his pure, masculine essence. His being takes me over and disintegrates all my defenses in a split second.

I collapse into that kiss and my body turns to melted butter in his hands. I sink on top of him and feel all the raging hardness from that night.

He tenses when he feels me on top of him. My hips arch toward him when his tongue swirls in my mouth. I'll never forget that tongue exploring all my inner secrets.

He responds instantly, grips my thigh, and pulls my legs onto either side of his waist. That position lights me on fire. I can't stop this.

His hardness swells between my legs and he flexes his hips to drive up into me from below. I'm wearing casual slacks and a button-up blouse. He's still wearing his suit.

My desire escalates so much faster this time than it did last time. My body knows him. My flesh understands exactly what he'll do to me and where he'll take me.

My body wants him a thousand times more than I do—which is a lot. I can't help moaning and whining when I feel his hardness between my legs.

He doesn't hold back or take it slow the way he did last time. He grabs me in rough handfuls, grips my ass, and drills me down on him while he spirals his hips upward to crush my sensitive tissues.

I yelp when he seizes my breasts through my shirt. He doesn't let go. He pinches my nipple hard enough to make me scream, rips his mouth away from mine, and bites me through my shirt and bra.

I cry out as a rush of exhilarating sensation spikes me out of my mind. He's going to do it this time. There's no stopping him.

The fear I usually feel turns to excitement. This is it. He's really going to do it.

Thinking that turns me on as never before. I want to grab him and pulverize him into myself, but he's already coming at me too fast.

He raises his head and consumes my mouth in monstrous kisses while his hands fly to the waistband of my pants. He flicks the button open and plunges his hand inside, but he doesn't go past my panties.

He flattens his fingers there, pulls away from my mouth, and stares up at me in smoldering fire while he rubs me to oblivion. "You want that?" he murmurs. "Huh? Do you want me in there?"

"Christophe...." I moan and my eyes roll back in their sockets as a surge of brutal desire blasts me out of my mind.

"Come on," he breathes. "You know you want me in there. Is this mine? You want me to take this? Huh? Do you want me to take this?"

I scream again when he starts circling faster. He's going to make me climax the way he did before.

I can't stop it. My body presses into him from my breasts all the way down to my quivering channel spasming to take his fingers inside.

He can already feel how saturated my panties are. He doesn't even have to ask if I want him.

He pulls me in and drowns me in his majestic kiss. I don't even try to stop myself from moaning in an agony of desire when I wind my flesh on his hand.

He doesn't stop. He controls my head with one hand and bumps his rock-hard knob up into me from below while he works me faster and faster.

I scream into his mouth and then succumb to a bone-crushing climax as he teases me to my limit. I jolt and thrash in his arms, but he only tightens his grip on me. He doesn't stop until I crumble onto his chest sobbing and whimpering in the throes of ecstasy.

Chapter 23: Geneviève

Christophe wraps his arms around me, kisses my hair, and settles down exactly where he was before. He doesn't have to do it with me. He could wait forever. He already owns my heart and soul—and he knows it.

He knows he can make me respond as no one else can. He knows I belong to him in ways I've never belonged to anyone else—and not because we're married.

He hugs my head into his chest and rubs my back. Giving me this unbelievable pleasure is all in a day's work for him. He doesn't need anything for himself. He sighs in perfect satisfaction just from feeling me tremble in his arms.

He definitely knows how to take my mind off things. All tension drains out of my neck, back, and shoulders. I can't move except to wrap my arms around him and huddle in the protection of his arms.

All the same problems are still out there, but I can't think about them anymore. I just have to trust Christophe and his brothers and cousins to handle it. I certainly can't.

Doing it with him like this doesn't answer the one question burning a hole in my mind.

I have to work hard to drag my brain back into some working order before I can get my voice to make a sound.

"Are you ever going to do it?" I husk.

He stiffens on the couch. "Do you want me to?"

Now I'm the one who hesitates. "I do. I'm just……" I hold onto him tighter and shut my eyes against his shirt. "I'm scared to."

He hugs me closer and kisses my hair again. "You know I would make sure you enjoyed it. Right? You know that, right?"

I'm too emotionally fragile to answer. I can only nod against his shirt. I want him more than anything. I don't want to be afraid of it anymore, especially not when I know he would be gentle with me.

He doesn't say or do anything for a long time. He probably never will. He doesn't want to be the one who crosses that line.

I really wish he would, but I can't be the one who starts it off. I need him to do that for me. I don't know why. I'm just not ready to initiate it on my own.

He finally pushes me off him. "Sit up here, baby," he tells me.

He guides me back on top of him and pulls my legs onto either side of his hips. He doesn't drill or pound up into me. He just lies there, completely relaxed.

He strokes my hair out of my face and then holds eye contact while he starts unbuttoning my shirt.

I give myself into his hands. He knows what I need better than I do. I don't know how to do any of this.

I gaze into his eyes. I trust him. I trust him with all that I am and all I have. I don't want anyone else to do this for me. I want him to be the one.

I feel more for him than I ever thought I could feel for anyone. I feel overpowering love, trust, and admiration for everything he is. I can't think of any better man to take my virginity.

I know he'll be careful with me. I know I'll enjoy it. He makes me enjoy it even when doesn't do it with me. He'll give me a thousand orgasms before he has a single one. He's been showing me that all this time. It won't change now.

He unbuttons my shirt and pulls it off so I'm straddling him in my bra. I don't feel the slightest bit of embarrassment that he's seeing me with my clothes off. I want him to.

He sits up, swivels into a sitting position on the couch with me still straddling him, and unclips my bra.

He makes every move with soul-destroying slowness. He glides my bra straps down and then nuzzles in to suck my breasts as soon as my bra falls away.

I dissolve in an agony of moaning and riding him as he nags me to a frenzy. I need him so bad! I can't go another day without him.

I run my fingers through his hair while he teases my nipples to hard little sensitive nubs. He plays with one between his fingers while he nibbles the other and makes me scream when I feel his teeth.

He crams my breasts into his mouth one after the other and growls to himself in animal madness. I try to pull his shirt off, but I can't do that when he's sitting on the couch.

He finally yanks it out of his belt, unbuttons four buttons at his collar, and strips the shirt off over his head.

He's wearing another pale beige T-shirt underneath his business shirt. He peels off the T-shirt, too, and throws them both away.

This isn't the first time I've seen him with his shirt off, but seeing him like this means something different now.

His muscled, chiseled shoulders infect me with their sensual appeal. He turns me on so much more, now that he looks so much wilder and more unchained.

He doesn't look like a prince. He looks like a raw slab of a man who sees what he wants and gets it.

His muscles bulge when he picks me up, pivots sideways, and lays me down on my back on the couch. He pushes my arms above my head so he can stroke my breasts and see me writhe and moan under his hands.

His eyes leave me nowhere to hide. He can see how much I want him—how much I'm giving myself to him with no reservations.

He slides both hands down to my waist to my hips and starts unbuttoning my pants. I want to spread my legs for him, but I have to bring my knees together so he can pull down my pants and my underwear with them.

He slithers them down my legs and leaves me lying naked in front of him. He looks even more powerful with his shirt off and me totally exposed in front of him. We both know what happens next.

He leans down and starts kissing me. I vanish into that kiss and fold my arms around his neck. I want to feel his bare skin against my body, but he snaps me out of my trance when he circles his fingers in my twitching mound again.

He pulls away from my kiss so he can look directly into my eyes while he drives me out of my mind.

I gasp and grimace as the escalating power consumes me. I can't look away from those eyes that command me to give myself to him, body and soul.

He quickens his pace. His bicep flexes when he presses in harder. His eyes demand to know that I'm his forever and always when I surrender to him like this.

He watches me pant and shiver and bare my teeth in primal insanity as he brings me closer to the breaking point. I spread my legs wider to feel a little more stretch under his fingers. I need more—a lot more.

He gives me one more kiss and crawls down me to bury his face in my saturated flesh. His tongue touches a jet of fire to my sensitive tissues and his fingers glide into my wetness.

I scream and then collapse in broken roars as he devours me to the heavens and back. He plunges his fingers deep inside me while his mouth breaks me open to let all the liquid gold of my emotion pour out.

His other hand grips me everywhere at once—my thigh, my hip, my breasts, my ass. He attacks me in animal fury, eats me to a screaming mess, and his hands split my body open.

I scream again and again as his fingers drive me into outer space. I'm falling apart in his hands the way I always do. He leaves me ragged and aching, but I'm only aching for more of him.

He stays down there a lot longer this time. I thrash and heave on the couch as one climax after another spikes me off the charts.

I'm just about to tell him that I can't take anymore when he drives a third finger into me.

The extra thickness blasts me out of my mind all over again. He lifts off me licking my juices off his lips and looks down at me in predatory fury.

I can't look away as he plunges his fingers in again and again. He doesn't slow down or ease off.

I spread my legs as wide as they will go. My body comes apart at the seams in one epic climax after another. I'm nothing but one ragged nerve skyrocketing away into the clouds again and again every time he thrusts into me.

His body swells with power. His arm thickens with the strain of taking me like this. Is this what he meant by taking me for his own?

I can only look up into those hard, unforgiving eyes and feel myself falling into his hands. Everything about me is his for the taking—not just my body. He must know that now.

He makes me look and see it happening. He doesn't let me look away or hide from the path my life is taking—because of him.

He's my future. He's my everything. Whatever happens to me will happen through him. I can't lose him now.

He scoops up my other leg and swivels it sideways to turn me over. I don't know where he wants me to go until he rolls me all the way over.

I come to rest on my stomach on the edge of the couch. One of my legs falls off so my knee lands on the floor. My other leg still rests on the couch cushion. This position spreads my ass and thighs for him with me lying on my chest and stomach.

He doesn't pull his fingers out—not for anything. He keeps corkscrewing them into me again and again and blasting me apart with one epic thrust after another.

He pivots off the couch at the same time, leans over me from behind, and drives his hips against his hand from behind.

He rests his hot, rasping mouth against my ear and pants in deep, husky, animal growls as he drives me to another catastrophic breaking point.

"Yeah," he breathes. "Oh, yeah. Take it all the way in. Take it nice and deep the way you like it."

I never thought I would like it like this. This position makes me feel shameless and animalistic. I want him to take me like this. I want him to plow me from behind and make me scream in ecstasy the way I am right now.

I throw back my head howling in broken roars as all these climaxes tear me apart. Will it never end? Will he ever take me and put me out of my misery?

Almost the minute I think that, his hot, throbbing, naked shaft touches my engorged slit down there. He doesn't take his fingers out of me.

He pumps against my ass and drags his length between my quivering wetness. He excites all my sensitive tissues.

My mind shifts gears again and I feel him taking me even though these are just his fingers. I feel him slamming into my ass from behind and spanking me into next week as we both release together.

I hear him snarling encouragement and commands into my ear, but I can't hear him over my own screams.

One word echoes in my shattered mind. *Please.* I need him to take me right now.

I need him to pull his fingers out and slide into me in their place. I need to feel his heat and his thick rod consuming everything in a shower of bliss.

Please. My whole being cries out for him, but he still doesn't do it. He teases me out of my senses—and then eases off. I almost cry in brutal desire, but he has other ideas.

He picks up my floppy body, turns me over, and lifts me back onto his lap where I was sitting before. He leans back on the couch so I'm straddling him.

He kisses me only for a few seconds while he strokes my cheeks and hair. "Sit down on me, baby. That's right. You're ready now. Sit down on me and take it all the way in."

I can't think well enough to resist. His words act on my mind with the power of a hypnotic spell. My body somehow knows what to do better than I do.

I start to lower myself onto his lap. I'm too out of my mind in all these delirious sensations. I can't stop what's about to happen. My body takes over and carries me somewhere even more mind-blowing than this.

He sticks his hand between my legs and holds his prick up in the right position. I don't even have to think.

He wraps his other arm around me to guide me down. His knob touches my slit and then presses deeper as my weight sinks onto it.

"That's right," he whispers in my face. "You want that so bad, don't you? Do you know how good that's gonna feel when you finally get it inside you? You can't live without it, can you?"

I groan and then scream as he presses just a little tighter. He won't push all the way into me until I do it myself. He can't push all the way in—not in this position. I have to break that barrier on my own.

I clutch at him with both arms. The tiniest trace of fear mingles with the drunken ecstasy of all the rapture he's giving me.

I can't hold myself up. My thighs weaken and my weight falls just a little more against his spike.

He's been stretching me so much with his fingers that he sinks in much more easily than I expect. I thought it would hurt and maybe tear my flesh apart, but it goes in with no resistance at all.

"Oh, yeah!" he breathes. "Oh, fuck, that feels so good, baby! You feel so good!"

I can't stop screaming as his thick shaft fills me to the breaking point. It feels so much better than his fingers. His heat overpowers me and I feel myself escalating out of control all over again.

I can't control my body anymore. I spasm and wind up falling all the way down onto his lap. His throbbing meat plunges to my deepest depths. I can't stop screaming and convulsing in his arms.

He takes over and uses his arms to draw me into a steady rhythm. The sensation of his shaft exciting all my sensitive tissues blasts me out of my mind.

I crush him in my arms holding on for dear life. I can't handle the intensity of all these sensations.

He keeps the same steady rhythm and never picks up speed, but I keep cycling higher with every stroke. Nothing can stop the cataclysm once it starts.

An epic wave of pleasure and power overtakes me and I crumble in his arms screaming and jolting.

He reacts instantly, scoots to the edge of the couch, and lowers his knees so he can thrust up into me from below.

He clamps one muscular arm around my waist and slides the other up to the back of my neck. He can guide my body where he wants it from this position.

He raises and lowers my weight in time to his pounding thrusts. He drills up into me from below, catches the wave, and propels it skyward even faster.

I can't stop reeling in the clouds of tormented bliss and catastrophe that crash me from one end of the universe to the other. I don't know what's happening to me, but he's the one who's doing this to me.

He slams me down on him so fast and hard that I can't take all the energy channeling through my being.

I hurl myself back in his arms. My body flies wildly in all directions, but he holds me in his powerful arms no matter what.

I hear him roaring out in broken fury as all that power pours into me and the world vanishes in that moment of togetherness.

Chapter 24: Christophe.

I drift out of a sound sleep and instantly smell the most heavenly aroma in my nostrils. I inhale deeply so I can get as much of that delicious smell as I can get.

I don't even have to open my eyes to recognize Geneviève's smell. Her trim, tight body lies limp and soft in my arms.

I bury my face in her hair to drink in that blissful smell. I'm still half-asleep, but that smell starts to turn me on in spite of myself.

She whimpers and squirms when she feels me starting to get hard. I curl around her body from behind. I should let her sleep, but my arms tighten around her in spite of myself.

I must have woken her up—or maybe she was already awake. She twists onto her stomach and starts kissing my face all over.

I don't open my eyes. We've been having so much sex all night long. I can't get enough of her, but she's probably sore and wants to rest. I know I am.

She strokes my hair and rubs my neck. Everything about her feels good. Lying here with her all exhausted from sex and sleep—it feels better than anything I've ever felt in my life. I don't want to move.

She slides her arm back under the covers and grabs my prick without warning. I groan when she starts stroking me even harder. She won't leave me alone.

"Baby...." I husk.

She whispers, "I need you," into my face. Who am I to argue with that?

She scoots closer to me, raises her thigh, and angles my meat so she can work herself down on me. She holds onto me while she pumps her body into me from the side.

Her heavenly channel wakes me up the rest of the way. I have to get that. I have to own it and conquer it.

This position won't let me. I heave off the bed and roll her onto her back.

She sprawls in front of me with her immaculate breasts swaying and her thighs spread for me to drive into her. I hold myself up on my arms so I can see her luscious white flesh bounce when I hammer her.

She raises her arms to hold me around my neck, kisses me, and then lies back with her arms above her head. God, she is so beautiful!

She's a thousand times more beautiful because she gives herself to me like this. She opens herself for me to unload all of myself into her. She holds nothing back from me.

She lets herself go soft and silky to receive all my hardness. Her joints liquify for me to pour so much love and desire into her.

All of that emotion comes back to me. I don't even have to ask how she feels about me. It's all right there written in her eyes.

She strokes my cheeks, grabs my ass and thighs, and presses her small, delicate hands against my chest as I build up power. I have to kiss her.

I sink on top of her and she wraps herself around me when I rest my weight on her. I crush her in my arms and feel myself building up to explode. She takes it all. She can take all that I am.

I hunger for her so much that I can't stop myself from sinking my teeth into her shoulder. Every morsel of her is endlessly delicious.

That one act of animal madness releases the inner demon in me. I slam into her full force. She screams in my ear in high, lilting cries as her channel undulates and compresses around me.

That feeling triggers me to explode. I pulverize her for a second before I collapse on top of her still spasming in the throes of ecstasy.

She sobs in my ear, runs her fingers through my hair, and writhes under me trying to screw her hips down on top of me.

I must have drifted off in that position because I snap out of a trance when Geneviève squirms again. I don't know how long I've been lying on top of her. I could have been sleeping there for hours.

She pushes me off and rasps, "I have to go to the bathroom."

I topple off her and collapse on the bed while she scrambles out and hustles across the room. The sun is coming up outside. It's morning, but I'm exhausted. I can barely summon the energy to lift my arm to rub my eyes.

She comes back, slips into bed all naked and succulent, and cuddles up next to me under the blankets.

I put my arm around her shoulders and start to drift off again. How have I been living my life all this time without this bliss?

My life is going to change after this. I definitely won't work as hard if I can come home to this every night. I'll have to spend a lot more time in the apartment with her.

She throws her head back, runs her fingers through her hair, and her husky voice drifts into my ear from a few inches away. "Don't you have to go do something important today?"

"Yes, I do. I have you to do today."

I rear off the bed, roll her onto her back, and kiss her while I weasel my hips between her thighs again. She laughs and then I catch a glimpse of her smiling at me. I find myself laughing, too.

I don't get off her, but the energy changes so I don't continue to the main event. God knows I've been doing enough of that since last night.

"Did I hurt you last night?" I ask.

She laughs at me again. "It would be a little late now if you did."

"Do I need to do a full medical examination?"

She bursts into blushing giggles. "Just don't start talking about doing any scientific experiments on me."

I ease farther down and start crawling under the covers. I don't stop smirking at her as I scoot down between her thighs. "I think I better check to make sure."

She laughs again. "Now I'm really worried."

I laugh, too, but she's smiling so happily that I don't stop. I work my way down there, spread her thighs, and tease her delicate, frilly petals out of the way.

"Yes," I murmur. "Yes, I think you definitely need some medical attention."

She giggles and then moans when I lick her. "Aargh!" she whimpers. "It's sore."

"Poor little flower." I give her a few more comforting licks. "I'll have to be gentle with you from now on."

"Don't you dare!" She mews again when I circle my tongue through her tissues and around her clitoris.

I glide one finger into her and make her sob in deep desire. One finger won't hurt her and she responds instantly.

She doesn't break eye contact. She holds my gaze and lets me see all the shades of deep bliss and emotion washing through her body and across her face.

I love seeing her like this. I love tearing aside the veil and exposing her deepest heart.

Her body sways and ripples in my hands every time I touch her. Her flesh trembles with so much life pulsing through her.

I want to make this body do so many things when I feel her quivering like this. I want to make this body become something. I want to make it become my future.

This is the body that will bear my children. I know that now. She's the one. She's my wife and that's the way she'll stay. We'll keep going and become something so much more than either of us ever imagined.

I get so fascinated by watching her that I forget to lick her. I prop myself up on my elbow and gaze down at her from above.

Her lips shiver and her nostrils flare when I finger her. Her eyes float in so much blissful desire until she smirks and asks, "What's the prognosis, Doctor?"

I find myself laughing and I flop onto the bed next to her. "I think you're going to live."

"That's good. I wouldn't want to miss out on any of this." She rolls against my side and strokes my chest and stomach. "Thank you for last night. It was everything I dreamed it would be."

I kiss her on the forehead. "Are you sure it wasn't as nightmarish as you dreamed it would be?"

She laughs. "I'm really glad I got it over with. Now I don't have to dread it anymore."

"As long as you don't dread doing it again....."

"Not at all." She kisses the side of my head. "I'm sure you know you were fantastic."

"Not as fantastic as you. You're beautiful. I love doing it with you."

She cuddles close to me extra tight and whispers, "Me, too."

I shut my eyes in the dreamy heaven of just holding her. This is somehow so much better than sex. The sex is just a prelude to this. This is the real stuff. This is where the real magic happens.

I want to wrap my body around her again, but I want to wrap my heart around her even more. I want to do it with her heart. I don't even know what that means, but that's the way I feel.

We both must be a lot more exhausted than I think, because I wake up hours later when someone bangs on the apartment door out in the living room.

"Christophe!" It's Dorian. "Are you alive in there?"

I pry my head off the pillow and look around in fuzzy confusion. The clock on the bedside table says it's eleven o'clock in the morning.

"I'm coming!" I choke. "Give me a minute."

I crawl out of Geneviève's arms. She curls up and falls back to sleep with her hair scattered all over her face.

I pretend not to notice her delicate white arm lying outside the covers. It flows to her bare back and ribs leading down to her waist and the rest of her naked body.

Is this what has been keeping me up at all hours of the night working—the fact that I didn't have this—this angel waiting for me in my bed?

I've had my share of girls. None of them made me want to come home and crawl inside them the way I want to crawl inside her.

I have to hustle out to the living room and pull my clothes on before I meet Dorian at the apartment door. He frowns when he sees me rubbing the sleep out of my eyes.

"Where have you been?!" he demands. "We've been working on the convoy situation. You should have come to the security office hours ago."

"Sorry, man. I had to catch up on sleep. I'll be right there."

He compresses his lips. This is the first time I've missed work in......well, forever. Does he suspect the reason why?

It doesn't matter. I'm married. I'm entitled to sleep in with my wife every now and then.

I make a few more pathetic excuses and retreat back inside. I don't wake up Geneviève before I take a shower, get dressed, and put myself together in a much more presentable condition to go out to meet Dorian.

He doesn't ask any other questions and I don't give him any explanation. He starts talking about the convoy. We're bringing in a specialist security team to take out the Lefebvres' hit squad.

"Our guys will get into position the night before," Dorian tells me. "They'll take out the hit squad before the convoy leaves Monaco. Our people should clean up the whole mess before we get anywhere near the location."

I nod. "It would be good if we could find out who the Lefebvres are hiring for this. Maybe we could neutralize them before the day."

"We're already looking into it through the Lefebvres' bank transactions and a few other channels."

We walk into the security office. My brothers and the rest of my cousins are already in there working with our usual security guys.

"We're also planning on sending through a decoy convoy," Pascal tells me. "The Lefebvres and their people will hit the first convoy, probably blow up a bunch of cars, and then the team will move in to extract Geneviève and finish off any survivors. That will give our guys a chance to put the assailants down before the real convoy goes through."

"So we'll have to leave the palace later than we planned," I point out. "We'll need to send word to Château des Gennennois that we'll be coming in late."

"We already did that," Renáld tells me. "It's all set up."

"So you don't need me after all." I turn to Casim. "Did you find out anything about Marcel showing up to the gala? Did you track him down?"

"We found the footage of him talking to Geneviève, but he disappeared right after that. He left the gala and now he's back with his father and Remi at their estate."

"His disguise was pretty good, too," Salvatore remarks. "We would never be able to prove it was actually him. It looks exactly like an old woman."

I frown at the diagrams spread out on the table in front of me. They're all floor plans for the palace. They don't help me at all when it comes to planning the convoy assault.

I cross the room to one of the computer stations. I bring up a map of the Provençale highway between Monaco and Nice. I locate the spot where Marcel said the Lefebvre team plans to hit the convoy.

This doesn't tell me anything, either, actually. Nothing can tell me what will happen in the future.

I'm just thinking it over when my father walks into the security office. I jump out of my seat and all the other men in the room stop what they're doing.

"Father!" I exclaim. "What brings you up here? This isn't like you."

He barely smiles at me before he lets his eyes sweep the room. He takes in all my brothers, cousins, and our security staff standing around watching and listening.

"I wouldn't normally come up here," he remarks. "I came to tell you that I just received an invitation from Silvain Lefebvre."

"An invitation?" Pascal asks. "For what?"

"It's for an official dinner party with just the two families—to commemorate Christophe's and Geneviève's wedding and also to celebrate peace between our families."

"That's preposterous!" Dorian snaps. "They don't want to make peace—not when they're planning this convoy attack."

"I agree with you," my father replies. "The dinner is scheduled for the night before our departure. The dinner couldn't come at a more significant time."

"Significant of what?" Renáld asks. "Is he manipulating us or is he sincere?"

"I'm certain this is a manipulation," my father replies. "He wouldn't spring this on us at the last minute—the night after we got a report that he plans to attack us. He's trying to throw us off."

"What are we going to do about it?" Casim asks. "What *can* we do about it?"

"I have no choice but to accept the invitation," my father replies. "We're all invited, so we have to make a good showing. Declining the invitation would humiliate him and could lead to outright hostilities."

"What could be more outrightly hostile than assaulting our convoy and trying to kill us all?" Pascal points out. "We're already at that point."

"He hasn't attacked us yet," I tell him. "We aren't even supposed to know about the attack. We can't let them find out that Geneviève told us. We have to play along right up until the minute one of his men opens fire on us."

"Exactly," my father adds. "We have to go and we have to make it look like we're at perfect peace now. There may be some mistake about this and he never intended to attack us in the first place."

"Then why did Marcel tell Geneviève that they did plan to attack us?" Salvatore asks.

"I can think of a few reasons," I reply. "Remi and Marcel might have come up with this idea to test her loyalty—to see if she would tell us what they planned to do. Silvain might not be involved in this at all."

My father waves at all of us. "Work that into your plans. Do whatever you have to do. Bring as much security to the dinner as you need to, but we have to go and we have to make it look like the security is there for some other reason than to protect us from the Lefebvres. I'm sure you can work that out for yourselves."

He leaves us with plenty on our minds. "I never met such a rotten bunch as those Lefebvres," Casim snarls.

"Geneviève isn't," Pascal points out. "This is the second time she's risked everything for us. I never imagined someone would go as far as this."

I can't listen to this. I get back to the computer and pull up the map of the highway. "None of that matters. We know how to handle security for the dinner. We just have to make sure we get all of our chess pieces in place so we can outmaneuver the Lefebvres first."

Chapter 25: Christophe

My family gathers in the vestibule inside the archway where we'll load into our limos to go to the dinner meeting with the Lefebvres.

Everyone is here—my parents, my sisters and brothers, all my cousins, my aunt, and Geneviève.

I ease close to her. She looks incredible in a body-hugging silver-grey gown with magnificent diamond jewelry.

She keeps undulating her hips from side to side trying to adjust her position inside her dress.

All the other women in here wear evening gowns, too, and all the men wear tuxes. This dinner is going way over the top considering we're all supposed to be friends now.

"Are you ready for this?" I murmur under my breath. "How do you feel about seeing your father and brothers again in a public setting after everything that happened before?"

She squirms again, but sticking her hips out from one side to the other only makes her look so much sexier.

"I don't mind seeing them as long as nothing happens." Her eyes dart around the room, but she barely sees any of the people around her. "You don't think they'll try anything at the dinner, do you? You said they were trying to make nice before the convoy attack."

"I don't see that your family would stand to gain anything by attacking at the dinner. Your father and brothers can deny any involvement if some random hit team assaults our convoy on the open highway. Your family can say they didn't know anything about it and someone else must have ordered the hit."

She nods. "That's what I think."

I want to put my arm around her and kiss her, but now isn't the time or the place. I take her hand and squeeze. "Stop fussing with your dress. You look fantastic."

She blushes and smiles up at me. "That's the problem. It's....it's stimulating."

I raise my eyebrows. "Excuse me?"

She turns bright red and dips her eyebrows. "You know what I mean."

"Does that mean you're going to be extra ready for me when we get back to the apartment?"

She giggles. "I don't think there is anything that will make me any more ready for you than I already am."

A lightning bolt of desire shoots to my guts when she says that, but the security team startles both of us into paying attention when they open the doors for us to go outside.

Security guards swarm all over the driveway. They surround the first limo for my parents to get in with Simone and Emeline. Then Geneviève and I get into the second limo with Pascal and Renáld.

The cars pull away. My aunt Marguerite, Dorian, and Johanne will get into the last limo with Casim, Salvatore, and Daphne.

Geneviève and I keep holding hands on our side of the seat. We sit facing my two brothers, but neither of them remarks or even looks at our joined hands.

No one acts like Geneviève and me getting closer is anything they didn't already expect. Maybe the fact that she keeps proving herself is finally convincing them that she's worthy of my affection.

I said I wanted to give her a chance to prove herself. Now she is. She's proving herself beyond anyone's wildest dreams. I know my parents and siblings approve of her—as more than just an arrangement.

She keeps looking out the window. I feel her nerves, but that's okay. She'll handle herself when she sees her father and brothers again.

I don't see any reason why she should ever wind up in a situation where any of them could confront her or anything like that. She probably won't even talk to them.

She'll be with me if she does. Her father and brothers won't say or do anything as long as any of the Royal Family is around.

This dinner is supposed to be a formal affair where everyone minds their best manners. Silvain and his sons will be more concerned than we are about maintaining appearances and being extra nice to everyone, especially Geneviève.

She keeps looking out the window in nervous agitation. I settle deeper into the seat. I have to be calm enough for both of us so she doesn't get too worked up. She'll stay calm as long as I stay calm.

The limo turns a corner and pulls onto another street. The convoy of limos has to go around a curved section of freeway on-ramp to get to the venue.

My parents' limo slows down. Our limo slows down to match its speed to the limo in front of that. I glance out the window to see where we are, and at that moment, a punishing boom goes off underneath the car.

The whole car slams hard to the left and throws me, Pascal, and Renáld against the wall. I wind up crushing Geneviève under my weight and she screams.

Another brutal concussion hurls the car upward off the ground. We all get jumbled together before the car smashes down on its roof with a splintering crash.

I flounder out of my dazed confusion and look around. Pascal drags himself off the ceiling of the limo's passenger compartment. Blood streaks down his distorted face. I can't tell how badly he's hurt.

Geneviève lies unconscious on her side with blood covering one side of her face. Her eyebrow, cheekbone, and jawline already look like they're puffing up.

I cast around for some way to get out of this car. The crash shattered the side windows, but the impact also compressed the roof. None of those window openings is wide enough for me to crawl through.

The crash flattened the limo's back window, the driver's compartment roof, and destroyed the windshield, but the driver's compartment safety cage protected it better than the passenger compartment.

The driver's compartment looks relatively intact. One of those windows will be wide enough for us to get out.

The driver hangs from his seat with his seatbelt still holding him in position. I can't tell from here if he's dead or alive.

I pull Pascal up. "We can get out through the windshield! We'll have to break the glass!"

"Get Geneviève!" He tells me and bends over to check Renáld's pulse.

Renáld starts to stir when Pascal touches him. I crawl over to Geneviève.

I almost hate to move her when she's hurt this badly, but I have to do something to help her. I can't leave her lying here. She could need serious medical attention—and I don't mean that kind.

I'm just about to pick her up in my arms. Carrying her won't be easy while I climb through the broken windshield, but I'm her husband. What else would I do?

I lean close to her to jam my arms underneath her when I hear gunshots outside. The stutter of machinegun fire echoes through the streets.

Pascal and I both freeze and stare at gunmen in black masks gunning through the streets to stalk down the convoy. I can't see if the attackers are going after any of my family members, but they are definitely coming toward this limo.

Pascal springs away from me. "Come on!" he yells. "We gotta get out of here!"

I bend over again to pick up Geneviève, but she startles wide awake in a heartbeat. God, she looks awful!

"Huh?" she mumbles. "What's going on?"

"We're under assault! Come on! We gotta get out of here!"

I grab her hand and try to pick her up to help her toward the driver's compartment. Pascal helps Renáld. Renáld looks stunned, but at least he can move around well enough.

They clamber into the driver's compartment. Pascal throws himself into the passenger seat, angles his body upward, and starts kicking at the broken windshield with all his might.

I pull Geneviève away, but she won't move. She stares in frozen horror at the gunmen outside. They swivel into position right outside the limo's rear window. They aim their guns straight through the window at me and Geneviève sitting there.

"They ambushed us!" she wails. "Marcel lied to me so they could ambush us tonight! They never planned to hit the convoy on the highway!"

"Forget about that!" I yell in her ear. "We have to....."

The guns erupt and bullets rip through the car. I dive on top of Geneviève and crush her under my body as metal shards, flying shrapnel, and broken glass pinwheel through the air.

She huddles under me screaming again and again. The gunmen pivot around the car on both sides.

I hear Pascal yelling from the driver's compartment. I look up there. He has succeeded in kicking out the windshield, but Geneviève and I don't dare to move to go up there. Going outside will only get us killed.

Two gunmen flank the limo on each side. They shoot directly into the driver's compartment. They can see that Pascal and Renáld aren't in here anymore. These men are only shooting at me and Geneviève.

The truth hits me between the eyes. The Lefebvres aren't trying to kill me. They're trying to kill Geneviève.

Did they find out that she killed Raoul—or that she told us about the convoy? None of that matters now. The gunmen will carve their way through this car. Then Geneviève and I will be trapped in here with no way out. I can't let that happen.

I look up toward the limo's rear window. It's the only way out and the gunmen aren't standing there anymore.

I push myself onto my hands to pull Geneviève over there. We might get hurt when we wedge ourselves through the crushed opening, but it's our only shot.

At that moment, more gunmen storm out of nowhere and the Royal family's security team opens fire on the assailants. The attackers spin around to defend themselves.

A massive gunbattle breaks out with men from both sides hiding behind the limos and other covered spots.

"Let's go!" I yell to Geneviève. "Pascal! Come on! Come this way!"

I pull Geneviève to the window. She keeps trying to duck for cover even though only a few stray bullets hit the car now. They don't hit near enough to put us in danger.

I get to the window first, flatten myself to the crumpled ceiling, and scoot as low as I can to get out of the car while I have a chance. More security people gather under cover from the gunmen.

Those security people hold out their arms to help me slide through. Broken glass tears my suit, but so what?

I stop outside the window and stretch my arms back inside to take hold of Geneviève. Pascal and Renáld crouch behind her waiting their turn to get out. Geneviève whimpers in terror, but she comes to me and lets me ease her closer to the opening.

At that moment, another colossal boom goes off somewhere on the other end of the car. It bumps the car upward off the ground and slams it down just as hard.

Pascal and Renáld both fly upward toward the seat and crash down onto the ceiling. The impact whips Geneviève off the ceiling, smashes her into the seat with brutal force, and she lands down on the ceiling, unconscious.

She doesn't lift her head or stir. She's out cold. I can't wait any longer. I don't know if the car is under assault again. I don't want to stick around to find out.

I dive back through the window, get myself stuck between the tight, razor-sharp metal edges, and gather her in my arms as gently as I can.

I have to pull and yank her to slide her through the window. Pascal and Renáld help me by pushing her legs and hips.

She slides out into my arms. I pick her up and turn around to get her away from the gunbattle, but the security team moves in and takes her off my hands before I can go anywhere.

The security guys grab me just as hard and hustle me away so fast I don't even get a chance to see them take my brothers out of the car.

Chapter 26: Geneviève

I try to pry my swollen eyelids open and wind up groaning when I see that I'm lying in a hospital bed. I collapse back on the pillow. The whole right side of my face feels three feet thick.

I catch a glimpse of two security guards armed with automatic rifles. They wear body armor and stand inside the room, one man on either side of the door.

The window gives me a view of more armed security guards blockading the corridor outside.

Christophe's soft voice drifts into my ear when he sits down on the mattress next to me. His warm, gentle hands press mine, squeeze my arms, and rub my body through the blankets.

"Lie still, baby," he murmurs. "You're going to be all right. You have a bad concussion and some really ugly bruises on the side of your face, but you're going to be fine. The doctors say you'll make a full recovery as soon as the headache goes away and the swelling goes down."

I try one more time to open my eyes. I want to see him, but I can't stand to open my eyes for more than a few seconds.

The light in the room stabs me in the head. I have to keep my eyes shut. "That's your nice way of calling me ugly," I grumble.

He chuckles. "Nice to see you're feeling better."

I turn my face away and finally open my eyes, now that I'm not looking up at the lights. I can get used to it enough to keep my eyes open now.

"My family tried to kill me." Those words come from a deep, forgotten place inside myself.

I know they're true the minute I say them. My family tried to kill me. My father. Remi. Marcel.

Marcel snuck into the gala in disguise so he could lie to my face and manipulate me into a situation where he, Remi, and my father could try to kill me. There's no other explanation.

Christophe squeezes my hand again. "I know, baby. I don't know if they found out about any of this or maybe they didn't need a reason at all. Maybe they realized that……"

I look up at him. "They realized what?"

He swallows once. His eyes overflow with some painful emotion. "That I love you, baby…." he chokes. "I love you and you love me. Maybe your family realized that this whole marriage was turning real between us. Maybe that's why they did it—because they understand that you weren't their double agent anymore."

I want to look away, but I can't. My throat constricts. "I love you!" I blurt out. "I don't want anything to happen to you!"

He dives in and kisses me, but he does it gently. "Nothing is gonna happen to me. I'm going to be around to give you medical examinations for a long, long time."

I try to laugh, but tears spring to my eyes instead. "I'm sorry, Christophe!"

"Why are you sorry? You're the one who got hurt. You're the one in the hospital…."

"I'm in the hospital because of you! I'm in the hospital because you saved me."

"Baby!" he murmurs. He keeps stroking my left cheek where he won't hurt me. He gazes into my eyes with all that overpowering emotion. He's been looking at me like that a lot these last few days. "You saved me, remember? If I saved you last night, then I was just balancing the books. I love you. I would never leave you in danger."

"And now your whole family is in danger!" I break down crying. My face hurts too much to cry, but I can't stop it.

"Shh!" he whispers. "Shh! None of this is your fault. We're married now. We'll stay together no matter what. It's our job to protect you from anything and everything no matter who it is. We never would have been ready for that ambush without your warning. We had enough armed security on standby so they could respond when we needed them. Your family would have caught us totally unprepared if not for your warning. You saved all our lives, including mine. We have you to thank for that. We would have seen the dinner invitation as a gesture of friendship if not for your warning. Never apologize for that."

He wraps his arms around me and holds me while I pull myself together. I don't want to break down over this. I want to be strong so I can support the Royal Family as much as possible.

This latest incident only proves that I need to commit to them. My father and brothers don't hold any power over me anymore. I belong to Christophe and the Royal Family now. There's no going back.

I already declared my loyalties by killing Raoul and then telling Christophe about my family's plans.

I don't regret any of it. I just wish it wasn't my own father and brothers that the Royal Family considers its enemies now. I really wish I wasn't related to the Lefebvre family at all.

Christophe straightens up and hands me a box of tissues so I can blow my nose. I try to pretend I didn't just have an emotional breakdown.

I look around at nothing. "Where are we?" I croak. "Which hospital are we in?"

He smiles at me and pets my cheek. "We're in the palace, sweetheart. This is the palace medical clinic. We have our own medical team. We don't use mainstream hospitals unless we have to, especially when we have security concerns about leaving the palace. You don't have to go anywhere. When the doctors say you're ready, I'll take you back to the apartment. You're safe and you're home."

Tears well up in my eyes all over again when I look down at my hands in my lap. Home. This palace is home for me now—the place I hated coming to.

I don't want to leave. I know everyone here. They accept me and respect me. None of these people is trying to kill me.

I believe Christophe when he says everyone in his family wants to protect me. They all understand the danger I'm in.

My danger is their danger. We share a common enemy. I don't consider anyone in the Royal Family an enemy now, especially not Christophe.

He hugs me when he sees me crying again. I just hope he understands why I'm crying. I hope he doesn't think it's because I don't want to be with him.

We're still sitting there with our arms around each other when the medical team comes in. One of them is a middle-aged male doctor in a white lab coat. He has a thick head of curly black hair, a thick black mustache, and wears thick glasses.

A bunch of younger, taller, more muscular medics come with him and a flock of nurses bustles around the room.

Christophe stands up when the doctor halts by my bed. Christophe doesn't let go of my hand.

"How are you feeling, my dear?" the doctor asks.

"My head is killing me," I mumble. "And my face hurts."

He smiles at me. "Are you experiencing any difficulty focusing your vision?"

"No," I tell him. "I can see just fine."

"Any ringing in the ears or tingling in the extremities?"

"No, nothing like that. I feel normal apart from that."

He bends over and squeezes the back of my neck from the bones under my ears all the way down to my shoulders. "Any pain or tenderness here?"

"No," I reply.

He then tells me to turn my head from side to side as far as it will go. He asks if I have any pain when I do that. I don't.

"Then I think you can return to your apartment and rest there. You don't need to stay here anymore. You can contact me if your pain increases or you need any medication to help you cope."

"I can cope just fine. I don't need any medication."

The doctor turns to Christophe. "The warning signs for head injury complications are projectile vomiting or any changes in level of consciousness. Take her straight to the Emergency Department if she becomes nauseous or difficult to rouse."

Christophe nods and says, "Yes, Sir."

The nurses come over with a wheelchair all set up for me. A stab of pain hits me in the head when I try to sit up. Christophe helps ease me off the bed and into the wheelchair.

It's a good thing I don't have to walk or function in any other way. I just have to sit here while the nurses wheel me out of the room.

I'm on the other side of the palace from the wing where I stay in the apartment with Christophe. I spot a few different members of the Royal family on my way through the more central parts of the palace.

They all stop what they're doing to watch me pass. None of them comes over to ask me how I am, but I see in their eyes that they're all concerned about me.

I don't have to worry about them anymore. They'll wish me well and thank me the next time they see me—whenever that is.

I can't even keep my eyes open right now. I need to lie down. Even sitting up is too challenging for me.

The nurses wheel me into the apartment and into the bedroom. I have to put my weight on my rubbery legs just long enough to swivel sideways and collapse on the bed.

Christophe pulls down the covers for me. I don't even stay upright long enough to thank the medical people for taking care of me and bringing me back.

Christophe does that for me, escorts them out of the apartment, and shuts the door on a blissful silence. I lie on the bed, not moving. All my limbs feel impossibly heavy.

I hear Christophe moving around the apartment out there. Then he comes in and sits down on his side of the bed.

"You don't have to hover over me," I mumble. "I'm just going to pass out for a while."

"Go ahead. I don't have anything better to do."

I snort and look away. "Now I know you're lying."

"I'll meet with the other guys later tonight. We have to decide what to do about the attack."

"What is there to do about it? It already happened. We aren't still planning to travel to Château des Gennennois, are we?"

"No, but we do have to do something about the attack." He turns toward me, rests on his elbow, and stares deeply into my eyes. "We have to retaliate. We have to send a message to our enemies—and not just our enemies in your family. We have to strike back—which means some more of your family members will probably get killed. How do you feel about that?"

I can't look at him. I don't want to look at anything. "I guess I can't argue with that."

"I don't want it to come between us. I don't want you to resent me for being a part of that."

"How could I ever resent you for it when my family just tried to kill me—and Raoul tried to kill you? Your family should have retaliated then. You have to do it now."

"I just want to make sure you understand and you're okay with it."

"Of course I'm okay with it! I want to help your family as much as I can."

His head shoots up. "You want to help?"

"Of course I do! Don't you know that by now? Isn't that what I've been doing all this time?"

He shrugs and sits up straight. "I guess so. I just didn't know you wanted to be a part of this."

"You actually thought I would want to leave my father, Remi, and Marcel alive out there to come after me and try again—and maybe succeed next time—and to leave René and Gabriel out there to carry on this feud afterward? Are you insane?"

"I didn't know you felt as strongly as that about it."

"Just finish it, Christophe! Finish all of them! I don't want to live in fear of them anymore—which is exactly what I will be doing if you leave even one of them alive. None of us will ever be able to stop looking over our shoulders thinking about them coming back. I would never feel safe. I would never have a life. I would never be able to leave the palace without fearing for my life."

He nods. "You're right. I'm glad you see it that way."

I sink back into my pillow. "Just tell me what you want me to do. I'll do whatever you want me to do—whatever I can do. Just don't ask me to do it today."

He leans over and kisses me on the temple. "I won't ask you to do anything until you're feeling better......not even this."

He squeezes my thigh hard enough and high enough to give me a sudden jolt of desire. I guess my head injury doesn't stop me from feeling that.

He only does it once and slips out of the room. I don't open my eyes. I really, really hope he's on his way to the security office to start planning this counterstrike. The sooner, the better.

Chapter 27: Christophe

I squeeze Geneviève's hand for the thousandth time to try to reassure her, but she doesn't need any more reassurance from me. God knows I've been giving her enough of it in the last few days.

She straightens up, squares her shoulders, and throws back her head to shake the hair out of her eyes before she faces the door to the palace security office. She already knows what she'll find inside.

I keep my grip on her hand and push the door open to lead her inside. My father, brothers, cousins, and our security team stand around the central table waiting for us.

They all turn around when Geneviève walks in. She's the fish out of water here.

Pascal and Casim pull back and everyone rearranges themselves to make room for us.

"Welcome, Geneviève," my father murmurs. "It's truly a pleasure to have you join us."

She barely looks at him or anyone else. "Thank you, Your Highness," she mumbles. "I just hope I can do something to help the family."

"You already have and you already are. We're all extremely grateful for your involvement."

She just says, "Thank you, Your Highness," again in a tiny voice.

The others turn to face the middle. "So the plan is to host another grand dinner party," I announce to the table at large even though my father, brothers, cousins, and I have already discussed this at length.

"We'll reciprocate your father's invitation by inviting your family to a celebratory dinner. This one will be intended to reschedule and reproduce the dinner your father invited us to. We're circulating around that we think the attack was carried out by one of the terrorist anti-monarchy groups in southern Europe. Your family has no reason to think we suspect them of carrying out this attack. We'll announce the dinner as a gesture of peace and friendship exactly the way they did."

"Unless they already know we suspect them," Dorian adds.

"We'll secure our route to a completely different venue through several different diversion points." I pull up a map on the table in front of me. "We'll be traveling in armored limos with our security detail riding alongside us. Once we get to the venue, we'll strike and finish off as many of the Lefebvres as we can. We'll put it around that the Lefebvres drew on us first and we retaliated in self-defense—which is true."

Everyone at the table turns around to look at Geneviève.

"Are you okay with that, my dear?" my father asks. "We don't want to offend you or upset you by having you involved in this."

"I have to be there," she insists. "They tried to kill me once. They won't be able to resist the temptation to try it again. I'm the bait to lure them into the trap. They'll be sure to accept when they find out I'm there."

"That's what we were hoping, but we didn't want to push you into something you weren't comfortable with," I tell her. "We can do this without you if we have to."

"I told you I want to be involved. I told you I want to help your family. This dinner is as much to celebrate our wedding as anything else. You and I both have to be there to show them how great it all is. Anyway, I can get closer to my father than any of you. I'll be able to get close enough to make sure he doesn't make it out of the venue alive."

The others gasp in horror. "You actually want to do that?!" Renáld chokes.

"You'll have to arrange with Lucille that I'm wearing an outfit that will allow me to take a weapon into the venue." Geneviève looks up at me. "I had a gun at the church. We could do something like that again—or she could sew some kind of pocket into the dress. I don't know."

I glance around the table. Everyone gawks at her in shock. None of us expected her to come out with an idea like this.

I could understand her wanting to kill Marcel after he lied to her and led her into that ambush.

She must be pretty certain that her father is behind this. I never dreamed she would want to kill him with her own hand.

My father puffs out his cheeks in a deep sigh. "I'm sure we can arrange for Lucille to adjust your outfit for that purpose, my dear—and I'm sure Christophe can arrange to give you an appropriate weapon for the occasion. We'll all be armed, so how you carry it out will depend on conditions at the venue."

She only nods. "I understand. I'm ready."

"You all know what to do," I say. "Let's start getting ready and make this happen. Then we can all go on with our lives and put this behind us."

The group breaks up. My brothers, cousins, and the security guys go back to work in the office. My father excuses himself and leaves.

I take Geneviève back to the apartment. "Why is everyone so shocked that I want to get involved in this?" she asks me on the way.

"We just want to make this as easy for you as possible—especially after how upset you got about Raoul. None of us wants to put you through that again if we can avoid it."

"We have to go to the dinner," she insists. "We both do. It would be even more important for me to go than for you to go."

"I understand that. We just want to protect you—from all of this."

She faces front and growls under her breath. "No one can protect me from this—not until they're dead."

I hesitate to ask, but I have to. "Are you certain your father is behind this? Are you certain the plan didn't come from your brothers?"

"I'm certain," she murmurs. "My father has executive power over the family finances. The team that carried out that ambush was a hired group of trained paramilitaries. They don't come cheap. Someone had to pay for it—which means my father had to sign off on it. He would want to know the whole plan. He would want to know exactly what the team was going to do. He would have known if the team set out to extract me and kill everyone else. He must have known ahead of time that the team had orders to kill me first."

I find myself shrugging. "I can't argue with that logic."

"You don't know my father," she mutters. "He knew about this if he didn't plan it himself. He was definitely involved in arranging this marriage. That didn't come from my brothers."

"Do you know if your father was the one who proposed the marriage idea to my father?" I ask. "I never found out which of them initiated the whole thing."

"The idea had to come from my father. Do you honestly believe your father would suggest to one of his sworn enemies that they marry their son and daughter to each other to bury the hatchet and make peace? Your father would never do that. He's the Crown Prince of Monaco. He doesn't need to do that. He's too high to make an overture like that to someone beneath him. He would have left the feud alone. The idea had to come from my father."

I don't know what to say. I don't know how she knows so much about my father, but she's right. My father is way too reserved to suggest the arrangement.

"Then do you think he arranged the marriage with the express intention of using you to strike at my family?" I ask. "Do you think that was his plan all along?"

"I don't see how it could be otherwise. Where along the line do you think he changed his mind if he didn't plan it ahead of time? He didn't set out to make peace and then suddenly completely reverse himself."

"What about when Raoul died? Maybe he changed his mind when he heard the report that Raoul died on the palace grounds—and the Renáld was the one who killed him—or when your father thought the Royal Family carried out a hit on Raoul. Maybe that turned your father against the whole idea of peace."

"My father already knew Remi and Raoul were against the arranged marriage. If my father really wanted peace, he would have considered Raoul's death a consequence of his own rash behavior. My father would have believed that Raoul acted on his own, broke into the palace grounds to harm the Royal Family, and he got caught. That on its own wouldn't have changed my father's mind about making peace if he really did want to make peace."

I wind up shrugging. We get to the apartment then and I open the door for her to enter.

She sits down on the couch. I shut the door, sit down next to her, and turn to kiss her. "Thank you for doing this," I breathe. "You have no idea how grateful we all are."

"Will you stop saying that?" she counters. "I'm the one who's grateful. Your family has been so kind to me—more than I deserve."

"You do deserve it. I never thought I would feel this way about someone I went through all of this with."

She squeezes my hand. "I'm the one who got lucky here. I'm just thankful I have your family to fall back on when this is all over." She passes her hand across her eyes. "I feel like I never had a family to begin with if they could turn against me like this."

I stroke her cheeks. Bruises still discolor one side of her face, but she looks normal now apart from that. The injuries from the assault are slowly fading away.

"I want to talk to you about something, baby," I tell her.

"What is it?"

"We need to talk about your fertility cycle."

She freezes. "What about it?"

"We need to talk about the possibility of you getting pregnant one of these days."

"I might already be pregnant. It isn't like we've taken any precautions when we did it before."

"How do you feel about that?" I ask.

"I'm happy about it. Did you think I had a problem with it?"

"I just want to make sure."

"I want to," she insists.

"You….you *want* to?" I blink at her. "Really?"

"Of course. I've always wanted children."

"But these wouldn't just be children. Our oldest son would be a part of the Royal Line. I would become Crown Prince after my father and our oldest son would become Crown Prince after me."

She waits for me to say something else. "And?"

"And...our children won't ever live a normal life. They'll grow up surrounded by security. They won't go to school. They'll spend most of their time in the palace. We'll have to take extra precautions with their security."

She only dips her chin once in a curt, short nod. "Of course. That goes without saying."

"So are you saying.....?" I find my hands migrating to her body. I stroke down her sides....and up..... "Are you saying you're okay....with us having unprotected sex......for the purpose of getting pregnant with our first child?"

Her lips pout open and her eyes glaze when I start stroking her breasts through her blouse. Her features shiver and her body wracks with tension.

I can't keep my hands off her when she responds to me like this. My other hand comes to rest on her thigh. I squeeze and glide up a little higher toward her hips.

"Do you want that, baby?" I murmur. "Do you want me to get inside you and make you grow?"

"Christophe....." she moans and whimpers in pathetic need when my hand slips between her legs to rub her through her slacks.

"Come to me, baby," I breathe. "That's right. You know you belong to me. That's right. You feel so good when I touch you like this, don't you? You are so beautiful."

Her eyes float half-shut and her cheeks flush with color when she rocks on my hand. She starts to shake and sag.

I pick her up and pull her onto my lap to straddle me. She holds onto me as she picks up my rhythm. Every squeeze of her breasts and ass, every stroke down her sides, every bite on her neck fires her into another reeling wave of ecstasy.

I can only sit here in awe of the power coursing through her. She rocks deeper into my hard knob. I plunge my hand into her panties and feel her wetness gush around me in deep, aching, saturated hunger.

My hand vanishes inside her—and then I vanish inside her. She'll receive my seed and grow whatever I plant in her soul. I'll give her as much love as I can and grow it into the biggest, most beautiful legacy this world has ever seen.

Chapter 28: Geneviève

I squeeze my hands on either side of my waist. The corset top of my elaborate gown cinches my waist extra tight before my hips flare out on either side at the bottom.

Christophe catches me adjusting my clothes—again. "Is it too tight?" he asks. "We can get Lucille to loosen it if you need to."

"No, it's comfortable enough. Besides, it has to be tight so everyone will be able to see that I'm not hiding anything underneath it."

He smirks at me, eases over to me, and slips his hand behind my back. He pulls me in close and rocks me against his body.

"What are you hiding underneath it?" he murmurs. "Maybe I should go down there and inspect."

I smirk back at him and wind up blushing. "We would never see you again if you did that."

His cheeks color and he pulls away just in time before his brothers enter the room. They're both wearing immaculate tuxes.

Pascal takes one look at me and his deformed features twist in a strange way. "You look stunning, Geneviève. That dress will definitely distract everyone from thinking about anything else."

I feel my cheeks burning. "Can we not talk about that?"

"Did I just catch you making a suggestive remark to my wife?" Christophe cuts in.

"Okay, can we please change the subject?" I interrupt. "I'm already nervous enough. Who's winning in the Rugby World Cup?"

"The cup is long over," Renáld chimes in. "Portugal won."

Dorian, Casim, and Salvatore enter the vestibule in time to hear the end of this conversation. "You need to keep up on current events," Casim tells me. "It's part of your duties as a member of the Royal Family."

"I'm sure it isn't part of my duties as a member of the Royal Family to keep up on every sporting event and team in the free world." I bend over to adjust my skirts. "Are you sure no one can see anything?"

"You were the one who insisted on changing the subject," Pascal interjects. "How can anyone tell if they can see anything if they don't look at you?"

I start turning red again, but Christophe comes to my aid. "No one can see a thing. You look perfect."

"How am I supposed to trust you?" I ask. "You wouldn't tell me if there was anything wrong with my outfit."

"I would definitely tell you if *that* was wrong with your outfit."

We have to end the conversation when the Prince and Princess come in with Simone and Emeline. Marguerite, Daphne, and Johanne show up a few minutes later.

The Crown Prince looks around at all of us. "Is everyone ready?"

Everyone nods. I squirm again.

The gun tucked into the garter under my dress burns a hole into my thigh. Its constant presence screams danger into my bloodstream, but this time is very different from taking a gun to my own wedding.

This gun lies tucked between my legs where no one will ever be able to see it. Just don't ask me what I'll do with it once the time comes for me to actually take it out.

The Prince and Princess face the doors leading out to the arch over the driveway. Everyone else takes their places and faces the doors, too. We're all ready to load up in the limos that will take us to the venue.

My father, Remi, Marcel, Gabriel, and René will meet us there. They and the Royal Family will act like the best of friends. Everyone will sit down to eat a celebratory meal and raise a toast to hail the peace between our families.

Then something else will happen. We won't sit there through the whole meal with nothing happening. The shit will hit the fan one way or the other—and I'll get caught in the middle of it.

Christophe elbows me from the side, whispers low, and adjusts the lapels of his jacket. "What about me? Can you see anything?"

I glance down at his jacket. He and all the guys are wearing sidearms in shoulder holsters under their suits. Most of them and the security guards are carrying plenty of other weapons in their back waistbands, around their ankles, and even in their pockets.

One is enough for me. I don't even know if I'll be able to use a gun against anyone in my family. I might freeze when the shooting starts—or one of them might kill me first.

Seeing my father and brothers again will be the deciding moment. I'll know the minute I lay eyes on them if they really had anything to do with almost getting me killed.

The doors open in front of us. The Prince and Princess walk outside to get into the limo.

I shake my head at Christophe and cast one backward glance at all the guys behind us. I can't see any of their weapons. Everyone keeps them perfectly concealed.

Christophe grabs my hand and we walk outside to get into the limo. We're riding with Pascal and Renáld again tonight—just like last time.

I catch both of them giving me significant glances on the way to the venue—and not because of the way I'm dressed. We've gone through this before. Nothing better happen on the way.

It's nice to know all three of these men would know how to handle it if something did happen. I couldn't be in safer hands—unless my family was off the streets. I'll never be completely safe until then.

Talking to Christophe about having children—it makes me so much more determined to go through with this. My children won't be safe as long as my family is still out there.

I could never put my future children in danger by leaving someone like that free to threaten my family. This has to end and it has to end tonight.

Having sex with Christophe means so much more, now that we both know where this is going. It can only end one way.

My desire for him knows no bounds, now that I made that connection. I need him and crave him inside me. I can't get enough of his seed and his primal essence flooding through me. I can't stop as long as he still has the strength and energy to keep going.

I can't start thinking about that—not now. I can't even look at him or I will start thinking about it.

I don't want to walk into the venue slippery wet and turned on thinking about Christophe getting me pregnant. I want to walk in cold, clear, and ironclad determined to end this one way or the other.

I don't have time to think about it before the limo pulls up in front of the hotel where the dinner will take place.

Christophe, the Crown Prince, and their security team decided to hold the dinner in a public venue so my father and brothers wouldn't be able to plant any extra gunmen ahead of time.

My father will only be able to bring the men who show up with him when he arrives. The Crown Prince also pulled strings with the hotel owners and managers to give us plenty of privacy. No one will disturb the proceedings.

Christophe pulls my hand through his arm on the way into the building. We exchange a knowing look. This is it—the moment of truth.

The Royal Family meets up in the lobby and we enter the dining hall set up with one long rectangular table.

A single chair sits at one end. Two chairs sit at the other end. Crystal, silver, and ornate candelabras decorate the table in between giant white flower arrangements and place cards.

My father, brothers, and cousins walk in mere seconds after we arrive. My father makes a big show of greeting the Crown Prince and all his sons.

My father spreads his arms and kisses the Crown Prince on the cheek. "So good of you to invite me!" my father exclaims. "Such a tragedy that happened last time."

He goes from Pascal to Renáld to Dorian. My father shakes hands with them and then stops in front of me.

"My darling dove!" He hugs me and kisses me on the cheek. "How radiant you look! Such a terrible thing those thugs did to you—but you still look as beautiful as ever."

He moves on to greet Marguerite. My father doesn't even stick around long enough for me to comment on his greeting.

I don't know if that means anything or if he's just trying to be formal because I belong to the other side now.

He comes to the end of the group and turns toward the table. "Sit down, sit down!" he exclaims like he's the host here instead of the

Crown Prince. My father seems to think he was the one who invited all these people.

The Crown Prince doesn't burst my father's bubble. Prince Gustav just goes along with my father's theatrics.

We approach the table and everyone arranges themselves according to their place cards. My father sits in the one chair at the end of the table. Prince Gustav and Princess Jasmine sit in the two chairs at the other end.

Christophe and I sit at the end of the table next to my father. Christophe's place occupies the very last chair on that end of the table. I sit next to him.

Remi and Marcel sit directly across from us. Gabriel sits on my other side. René sits on Marcel's other side across from Gabriel.

All the planning the Royal Family has put into this—it all comes together in my mind.

If my father was the one who arranged this table, I would definitely consider this suspicious. I would think my father was trying to trap me here away from every other member of the Royal Family.

Christophe is here, though, and my father didn't arrange the table. The Crown Prince did.

Is there a reason he put me right next to my father—and surrounded by my brothers and cousins? There always has to be a reason behind everything the Royal Family does.

Then again, maybe Christophe was the one who decided on the place settings. Pascal, Renáld, Dorian, Casim, and Salvatore sit in the next places down the table outside my cousins.

Pascal, Renáld, and Dorian sit on René's side. Casim and Salvatore sit on Gabriel's side. All the women in the Royal family sit at the other end of the table with my sisters Marina and Cécile. Not a single male sits at that end of the table except for the Crown Prince.

Now I know Christophe was the one who planned this. He wants the women to be able to get out of danger once the shooting starts. He doesn't want to harm them.

He pulls my chair out for me to sit down. I get a sick feeling in my stomach when my father sits down at the end of the table right next to Christophe.

How did I start hating my own father so much? I don't want him anywhere near Christophe.

Gabriel sits down next to me. I always considered him another big brother, but something about him doesn't feel right, either.

The whole table and dining room charges with crackling energy. Something is about to start.

One glance around the table confirms the truth. Everyone on the Lefebvre side knows what this dinner is about, too. They didn't buy the story about the anti-monarchists.

I don't see my brothers or cousins carrying a weapon, but they must be. They wouldn't come unarmed, especially if they plan to strike the first blow.

Maybe that's what this is all about. Maybe my family still thinks the Royal Family is in the dark. Maybe my father and brothers plan to hit the Royal Family unawares and wipe out everyone in one blow the way Marcel said they would.

I glance over at my father and he glances at me at the same moment. I see it all written there in his hard blue eyes. He's the one who did this. He married me to Christophe so my father could strike a fatal blow to the Royal Family.

I look down at my plate so I don't give too much away. What should I do about this?

The gun accuses me. Did I really come here to kill my own father? How can I go as far as that? That would make me no better than him.

Christophe squeezes my hand under the table. His eyes speak volumes to me from just inches away. Did he see that look passing between me and my father?

Christophe will always accept me. He won't hold it against me if I can't use the gun. He must understand that I would have mixed feelings about getting involved in this.

My presence alone makes it possible for the Royal Family to get into the same room with my father and brothers. Isn't that enough?

I can't answer any of those questions. I don't get a chance to before the servers enter and start laying out the main course. No one does anything or can do anything as long as the servers are in the room.

They serve everyone salad, leave the room, and we all start eating. What will be the trigger that ruins this supposedly tranquil atmosphere?

The room buzzes with barely concealed hostility. Everyone in the room holds themselves on tenterhooks. I don't know if I can take much more of this tension.

My father talks casually to Christophe about the world political situation. Anyone looking at them would think they were a loving father-in-law and son-in-law.

Remi and Marcel talk about some obscure soccer match I've never heard of taking place somewhere in Southeast Asia. Gabriel and René talk across the table about some repairs the maintenance staff is doing on my father's house.

Something is going wrong with the repairs. Gabriel wants to fire the company doing it and hire someone else. René thinks the family should give the current company more time to get it right and fix their mistake.

I don't talk to anyone. I secretly thank heaven that all the other women are sitting at the other end of the table. I couldn't talk to anyone right now to save my life.

The servers come back in, remove the salad plates, and serve soup. I glance down the table just as Pascal glances up and catches my eye. The main course is the signal for the Royal Family to strike.

Everyone is supposed to wait for the servers to lay out the main course. Then the door will close and everyone will....do whatever.

I still don't know what I'll do. I'll probably wind up hiding under the table until the shooting stops.

I bend over my bowl to spoon the soup into my mouth. I barely touch the spoon to my lips before Gabriel rockets out of his chair, hooks his elbow around my neck, and leaps away dragging me with him.

I scream, but he only clamps his arm tighter around my throat. He shoves a handgun against the side of my head while he hauls me backward away from the table.

"Nobody move!!" he roars. "Everyone stay where you are!! Don't try anything or the bitch gets....."

I struggle to free myself, but he's too strong. I can't breathe.

Lightning quick, before Gabriel even finishes saying his threat, Christophe materializes behind Gabriel and shoots him straight in the head.

Gabriel goes down like a ton of bricks and takes me with him. I get tangled up in his beefy arm. It clamps tighter around my neck when Christophe shoots him.

I can't get away. Gabriel and I both hit the floor and the whole dining room explodes in gunfire behind my back. I can't even see where Christophe is.

I flounder to pry Gabriel's arm off my neck. Half his head is gone. He will definitely never harm or threaten anyone again.

I flop out of his hold and land on my hands and knees on the floor. The corset bodice of this dress makes it especially hard to move around—not without my breasts flopping out of my bra.

I raise my head to try to find a safe place to hide, but at that moment, my father lunges out of nowhere, grabs my wrist, and drags me away.

He forces me to my feet and yanks me across the room, away from the table, toward another door on the opposite side of the dining hall. I don't know where that door goes.

I try to pull out of his grip. "Let me go, Papa!" I shriek. "Leave me alone!"

"Come on!" he bellows over his shoulder. "You're coming with me NOW!!"

I struggle a little harder, but he crushes my wrist in a bone-breaking hold. He keeps yanking me nearly off my feet.

He completely ignores my screams of pain and protest. He throws open the door and tows me into a long, narrow, grungy corridor leading away from the dining room.

That's the moment when I realize what he didn't say. He didn't say he had to get me away from the gunbattle to save me from all the flying bullets. He didn't say he had to get me away from the Royal Family to save me from this arranged marriage.

He only said I had to go with him. Is he the one who's going to kill me? Is that the whole point of this? Is he taking me to the hidden location where he plans to kill me?

The gun bumps into my thigh when I try to walk too fast. I stumble, but he only tugs me harder.

He yanks my arm so hard that he pulls me off balance. I trip and sprawl on the floor outside another door. He pulls out a set of keys and starts jingling them to find the right key to unlock the door.

I don't know where he's taking me or what he plans to do once he gets there, but it won't be anything good.

I push myself to my feet. He tries one of the keys, but it doesn't work. He has to try another one. I see it all. He must have gotten the key to this door just in the last couple of days—after he got Prince Gustav's invitation.

My father set this whole thing up so he could get me away from the Royal Family—but not so he could do anything good to me. Of course not.

He has to give up on the second key and try a third one. This could go on for a while. Maybe he stole that key ring from one of the hotel maintenance people. Maybe my father doesn't even know which key will open that door.

All my doubts evaporate. I know what I have to do. I can't let this man walk out of this hotel alive. My whole bright future with Christophe depends on ending this right now.

I pull the gun out from under my skirts, grasp it in both hands, and aim it at my father. He doesn't notice. He still has his back to me.

He tries one key after another. This could take all night.

"Turn around, Papa," I murmur.

He spins around and glares at me. Then his eyes dip to the gun.

"You hired those men to attack the limo convoy," I murmur. "You paid those men to try to kill me. Admit it."

"You stupid cow!" he snaps. "You're too soft in the head to carry out my plan on your own. You should have been tougher. You should have killed Christophe when you had the chance! Then I wouldn't have had to set him up to make it look like he killed you! You ruined my whole plan by being a soft, stupid girl instead of the woman I needed you to be! You betrayed your own family! You're no daughter of mine."

He looks down at the keyring, frowns, and starts going through the keys one at a time. He scowls at each one like he's trying to remember which key he's supposed to use.

I stand there in silence holding him at gunpoint. He completely ignores me.

Those words gouge into my brain. He was the one who set up Raoul to give me that gun. My own father was the one who wanted me to kill Christophe. The idea never came from Raoul or Remi at all.

My father set up Raoul to kill Christophe because I couldn't go through with it. My father did all of this—because he hates me.

I command myself again and again to pull the trigger, but I can't. Some force outside myself stops me. What if he's right about me? What if I'm too soft and weak to do anything?

What if I'm too soft and weak to protect my own children? What kind of mother would I be if I didn't protect them, especially from a monster like this?

My father would be the first person to demand to see my children. He would play the grandfather card and weasel his way into our lives so he could infect my new family with his poison the same way he infected the last one.

I can't let that happen, but I can't pull the trigger, either.

He compresses his lips, puts the keyring down, and sees me still standing there in turmoil. He takes one step toward me and raises his hand to grab the gun out of my hand.

I make a snap decision, jerk the gun up, and shoot straight into his eye socket. His head whips back from the impact and he topples back to slam down flat on his back on the floor.

I stand there staring at the body while it twitches and jolts in its death throes. Good. He's dead.

Smoke comes from the end of the gun. The tension in my arms evaporates and I lower the gun, but I can't slacken my grip on it—not for anything.

I'm still standing there in stunned disbelief when Christophe, Dorian, and Pascal come running down the corridor behind me. They slow and then stop when they see my father lying there dead at my feet.

"Are you okay?" Christophe whispers.

I can only nod in a numb trance. It's over. He's dead. He'll never interfere in my life again.

Christophe nods to his brother, takes the gun out of my hands, and passes it off to Pascal. Christophe puts his arm around my shoulders, turns me away from my father, and steers me back up the corridor going somewhere.

We exit through a different door and walk out of the building into a dim, cramped alley full of dumpsters and trash. Christophe hustles me to the end of the alley where a limo pulls up in front of us.

He pushes me into the back, climbs in with me, and the limo takes off at high speed. It doesn't stop until it skids into the driveway under the arch at the Royal Palace.

Christophe gets out first. We're all alone here with not a single security guard in sight. They're all back there at the hotel.

Christophe takes my hand, helps me out of the car, and hurries me down the palace's empty, echoing corridors to our own apartment.

He shuts the door, locks it, and folds me in his arms. I shut my eyes against his shirt and feel all my nervous tension coming out in trembling quivers all over my body. It's over. No one will ever bother us again.

End of Book 1.

Keep Reading

Royal House Series: Book 2: Under Guard

The last thing Princess Simone of Monaco needs is some sweaty gorilla bodyguard shadowing her every move, telling her what to do, interfering with her social schedule, and blocking her from interacting with her adoring fans. She vows not to let spiraling security concerns derail her life or the following she's worked so hard to build.

Her whole world will come to a screeching halt when her brother Prince Christophe hires a new bodyguard for her—and just in time. Alexei Asatiani is like no one else Simone has ever met—and she'll need all his skill and experience to survive the enemies moving in on her and the Royal Family.

The man she thought was her worst nightmare will become the one thing standing between her and ultimate disaster—so what will happen if she loses him in the line of fire just when she needs him the most?

You can find it at your favorite book retailer.

Sign Up Once--Get all A.E. Moran's free books including brand new releases

The last thing Princess Simone of Monaco needs is some sweaty gorilla bodyguard shadowing her every move, telling her what to do, interfering with her social schedule, and blocking her from interacting with her adoring fans. She vows not to let spiraling security concerns derail her life or the following she's worked so hard to build.

Her whole world will come to a screeching halt when her brother Prince Christophe hires a new bodyguard for her—and just in time. Alexei Asatiani is like no one else Simone has ever met—and she'll need all his skill and experience to survive the enemies moving in on her and the Royal Family.

The man she thought was her worst nightmare will become the one thing standing between her and ultimate disaster—so what will happen if she loses him in the line of fire just when she needs him the most?

Sign up at www.authoraemoran.com to read it for free.

About AE Moran

A .E Moran is the contemporary romance pen name for Theo Mann.

I write 70 books per year—and yes, before you ask, all these books are my original creative work. Nothing written under my name is AI-generated or ghostwritten because I write better than AI and any ghostwriter out there.

People don't read fiction for entertainment or to escape from reality. People read fiction to see their humanity reflected in another person's character and story.

This is my promise to you. When you read my books, you'll see your own humanity reflected in the characters and stories. I take this commitment to my readers very seriously. My books are an intimate form of communication between us. I would never disrespect my readers by turning that over to a machine or another writer. This is my bond between me and you as my reader.

I write 20,000 words per day as my daily work output. If anyone with a public platform would like to challenge me to prove this in a controlled environment, feel free to contact me on this website's contact page. How do I do write so much? Find out more on my blog, *Crimes Against Fiction* at www.theomann.com.

I worked as a professional ghostwriter for fifteen years. Now I'm going for the Guinness World Record by writing 700 books over the next ten years and 1400 books over the next twenty years, all originally written by me.

See my website for the full book list. I'm also the author of *Proof for the Existence of God* and the *Crimes Against Fiction* blog.

You can find out more at www.theomann.com or at www.author aemoran.com.

Also by AE Moran (so far)

www.ingramcontent.com/pod-product-compliance
Lightning Source LLC
Chambersburg PA
CBHW072226190626
46809CB00017B/890